ZIGZAGGER

Latino Voices

General Editor
Ilan Stavans

Editorial Board
Francisco Goldman
Achy Obejas
Judith Ortíz-Cofer
Johnny Payne

ZIGZAGGER

Manuel Muñoz

LATINO
VOICES

Northwestern University Press
Evanston, Illinois

Northwestern University Press
Evanston, Illinois 60208-4210

Printed in the United States of America

10 9 8 7 6 5 4 3 2 1

ISBN 0-8101-2098-4 (cloth)
ISBN 0-8101-2099-2 (paper)

This is a work of fiction. Characters, places, and events are the product of the author's imagination or are used fictitiously and do not represent actual people, places, or events.

LIBRARY OF CONGRESS CATALOGING-IN-PUBLICATION DATA
Muñoz, Manuel.
Zigzagger / Manuel Muñoz.
p. cm. — (Latino voices)
ISBN 0-8101-2098-4 (cloth : alk. paper) — ISBN 0-8101-2099-2 (pbk. : alk. paper)
1. Central Valley (Calif. : Valley)—Fiction. I. Title. II. Series.
PS3613.U69 Z54 2003
813'.6—dc21
2003010038

The paper used in this publication meets the minimum requirements of the American National Standard for Information Sciences—Permanence of Paper for Printed Library Materials, ANSI Z39.48-1992.

Book design by Jason Harvey

This book is for my sister, Elisa, who stands tall.

The exit is through Satan's mouth.

Sharon Olds, "Satan Says"

CONTENTS

ACKNOWLEDGMENTS

Grateful acknowledgment is made to the editors of the following journals in which many of these stories have appeared: *Blithe House Quarterly* ("Everything the White Boy Told You"); *Boston Review* ("Monkey, Sí"); *Colorado Review* ("Zigzagger"); *Epoch* ("Good as Yesterday"); *Fourteen Hills* ("Skyshot"); *Glimmer Train Stories* ("Anchorage" and "Campo"); *Many Mountains Moving* ("Not Nevada"); *Massachusetts Review* ("The Unimportant Lila Parr"); *Mid-American Review* ("Museo de Bellas Artes" and "*Tiburón*"); and *Puerto del Sol* ("The Third Myth").

"*Astilla*," "*Clima*," "*Fotito*," "Loco," and "The Wooden Boat" first appeared as *Greetings from Ice Country,* Chicano Chapbook Series, ed. Gary Soto, no. 19 (Berkeley, Calif.: Chicano Chapbook Series, 1998).

I give thanks to (and for) my early teachers, Don Milliken, Robert Heilmann, and Dawn Swift, for the gift of Gary Soto's *Black Hair;* to Susan Dodd and Jill McCorkle, for their gracious guidance while at Harvard; to the generosity of Cornell University's creative writing program, especially Ken McClane; to John Garza, Nhan Trinh, and Brennen Wysong, for giving their time to this work; and to the Constance Saltonstall Foundation for the Arts, for providing financial support so I could finish these stories. I offer my humble gratitude to Helena María Viramontes, who has led me by example.

ZIGZAGGER

·ANCHORED

Zigzagger

By six in the morning, the boy's convulsions have stopped. The light is graying in the window, allowing the boy's bedroom a shadowy calm—they can see without the lamp, and the father rises to turn it out. The boy's mother moves to stop him and the father realizes that she is still afraid, so he leaves it on. The sun seems slow to rise, and the room cannot brighten as quickly as they would like—it will be cloudy today.

The father is a bold man, but even he could not touch his teenage son several hours ago, when his jerking body was at its worst. The father makes the doorways in their house look narrow and small, his shoulders threatening to brush the jambs, yet even he had trouble controlling the boy and his violent sleep. And it was the father who first noticed how the room had become strangely cold to them, and they put on sweaters in the middle of July—the boy's body glistening, his legs kicking away the blankets as he moaned. The mother had been afraid to touch him at all and, even as the sun began rising, still made no move toward the boy.

In the morning light, the boy seems to have returned to health. He is sleeping peacefully now; he has not pushed away the quilts. His face has come back to a dark brown, the swelling around the eyes gone.

"I'll check his temperature," the father tells the mother, and she does not shake her head at the suggestion. She watches her husband closely as he moves to the bed and reaches for the edge of the quilt. She holds her breath. He pulls the quilt back slowly and reveals their son's brown legs, his bare feet. He puts out his hand to touch the boy's calf but doesn't pull away his fingers once he makes contact with the skin. The father turns to the mother, his fingers moving to the boy's hands and face. "I think he's okay now."

The mother sighs and, for the first time in hours, looks away from the bed. She remembers that today is Sunday and, with the encouragement of the coming morning, she rises from her chair to see for herself.

Saturdays in this town are for dancing. The churchgoers think it is a vile day, and when they drive by the fields on their way to morning services, they sometimes claim to see workers swaying their hips as they pick tomatoes or grapes. They say that nothing gets done on Saturday afternoons because the workers go home too early in order to prepare for a long night of dancing. It is not just evenings, but the stretch of day—a whole cycle of temptation—and the churchgoers feel thwarted in their pleadings to bring back the ones who have strayed. They see them in town at the dry cleaners or waxing their cars. They see them buying food that isn't necessary.

The churchgoers have war veterans among them, some of whom serve as administrators for the town's Veterans Hall. They argue with each other about the moral questions of renting out their hall for Saturday's recklessness. The war veterans tell them that theirs is a public building and that the banquet room, the ballroom, and the wing of tidy classrooms are for all sorts of uses. Sometimes the veterans toss out angry stories about Korea, and the more civil of the lot mention how they converted villagers while fighting. But others claim freedom, including their hall, and to mortify the churchgoers, they tell tales of Korean girls spreading their legs for soldiers and the relief it brought. The churchgoers end the conversation there.

By Saturday afternoon, there is always a bus from Texas or Arizona parked in back of the Veterans Hall, and sometimes workers on their way home will catch a glimpse of the musicians descending from the vehicle with accordions and sequined suits and sombreros in tow. Some days it is simply a chartered bus. But other times, it is a bus with the band's name painted along the side—CONJUNTO ALVAREZ, BENNIE JIMÉNEZ Y FUEGO—and the rumor of a more popular group coming through town will start the weekend much earlier than usual. It means people from towns on the other side of the Valley will make the trek. It means new and eager faces.

The churchgoers smart at the sight of young girls walking downtown toward the hall, their arms crossed in front of their breasts and holding themselves, as if the July evening breeze were capable of giving them a chill. For some of them, these young girls with arm-crossed breasts remind them of their own daughters who no longer live in town. They have moved away with babies to live alone in Los Angeles. All over town, the churchgoers know, young girls sneak from their homes to visit the friends their parents already dislike. There, they know, the girls put on skirts that twirl and makeup that might glisten against the dull lights of the makeshift dance floor. These girls practice walking on high heels, dance with each other in their bedrooms to get the feel in case a man asks them to do a *cumbia*. The churchgoers remember when they were parents and listening to the closed doors and the girls too silent. Or their teenage boys, just as quiet, then leaving with their pockets full of things hidden craftily in their rooms.

And much of this starts early in the day: the general movement of the town, the activity in the streets and shops—women buying panty hose at the last minute, twisting lipsticks at the pharmacy in search of a plum color. Men carry cases of beer home to drink in their front yards. Pumpkin seeds and beef jerky. Taking showers only minutes before it is time to go.

Saturdays in this town are for dancing, have always been. This town is only slightly bigger than the ones around it, but it is the only one with a Veterans Hall, big enough to hold hundreds. By evening, those other little towns are left with bare streets, their lone gas stations shutting down for the night, a stream of cars heading away to the bigger town. They leave only the churchgoers and the old people already in their beds. They leave parents awake, listening for the slide of a window or too many footsteps. They leave the slow blink atop the height of the water tower, a red glow that dulls and then brightens again as if it were any other day of the week.

For a moment, the mother does not know whether to go to the kitchen herself or to send her husband. She does not want to take her eyes away from her son and yet at the same time is afraid to be alone with him. She says to her husband, *"Una crema,"* but doesn't move toward getting the items she needs to make a lotion for the boy. She needs crushed mint leaves from the kitchen. She needs oil and water, rose petals from the yard.

"Do you want me to go?" her husband asks her. On the bed, the boy is sound asleep, and the sight of him in such a peaceful state almost makes her say yes. But she resists.

"No," she tells her husband. "I'll go."

She is sore from so much sitting, and the tension of having stayed awake makes movement all the worse. The rest of the house seems strangely pleasant: the living room bright because it faces east, the large clock ticking contentedly. She wishes she could tell her husband what to do, but she knows they cannot call a doctor and have him witness this. She has considered a priest, but her husband does not go to church. In the face of this indecision, the calm rooms in the rest of the house frustrate her. She wants to make noise, even from simple activity. From the kitchen, she takes a large bowl and searches her windowsill for a few sprigs of mint. She sets out a bottle of olive oil and a cup of cold water from the faucet.

In the front yard, where the roses line the skinny walkway to their door, the day is brighter than it appeared through the windows. It is overcast, but not a ceiling of low clouds, only large ones with spaces in between, and she can see how the sun will be able to shine through them. They appear to be fast-racing clouds, and, once the sun is high enough, they will plummet the town into gray before giving way to light again. Though slight, the day erases the fear in her.

She notices the skinny walkway and the open gate where their son stumbled home, the place where he vomited into the grass. She had watched from the living room window, his friends behind him at a far distance, dark forms in the street, and she had waited for them to go away as her son entered the house, cursing terribly. From her rose-bushes, she notices a gathering of flies buzzing around the mess, some of it on the gray stone of their walkway. There's a streak of red in it, she can see. She quickens her pace with the rose petals when the breeze comes up and the smell of the vomit in the grass lifts, reminding her of how ill her son was only hours ago. Dropping the petals into the bowl, she hurries back into the house, trying to get away from that smell.

She is crying in the kitchen, mixing the mint and the oil and the water, and to make it froth, she adds a bit of milk and egg. The concoction doesn't seem right to her anymore, doesn't match what she recalls as a young girl, her grandmother taking down everyday bottles from the cabinets and blessing their cuts and coughs. The mother does it without any knowledge, only guessing, but it makes her feel better despite feeling lost in her inability to remember. She takes the bowl into the bathroom and dumps half a bottle of hand lotion into the bowl, and the mix turns softer and creamy.

Back in the bedroom, her husband is still at their son's bedside, but the boy has not moved. The stale odor of the room reminds her again of outside and the earlier hours and her son's vile language and her husband's frantic struggle to keep the boy in bed, wild as he was. The boy tore off his own clothes, his thin hands ripping through his shirt and even his pants, shredding them, and he stalked into his bedroom naked and growling and strong. Her husband came to tower over him, beat him for coming home this way. The fear crept into her when the boy fought back and challenged and then, only by exhaustion, collapsed on the bed. He was quiet. And then the odor came. The smell was of liquor at first, but then a heavy urine. Then of something rotting. Her husband had yelled at her to open the windows. Even now, the smell lingers in the air.

"He's still sleeping," her husband whispers. "What do you have there?"

"A cure my grandmother used to give us," she says, half expecting her husband to ignore her and the bowl.

"You want to put it on him?" he offers, and she knows that her husband is asking whether or not she is still afraid.

She does not answer him but moves to the bed, setting the bowl on the floor. With her fingertips, she dips into the concoction and then, resisting an impulse to hold her breath, rubs it on her son's bare legs. They are remarkably smooth, and she looks at her husband as if to have him reassure her that what she had seen last night had not been an illusion. Her son's legs are hairless and cool to the touch. There are no raised veins. They are not reddened with welts. They are not laced with deep scratches made with terrible fingers.

The boy spent the early part of Saturday evening with a group of friends, all of them drinking in the backyard at the house of a girl whose parents were visiting relatives in another town. Even before the sun had set, most of the boy's friends had already had enough to drink, and they tried to convince some of the older boys to go back out and buy beer. But by then, the girls put a stop to all of it, saying the hall wouldn't let them in if they smelled beer on them.

The boy liked being with these friends because he did not have to do much. He laughed at other people when the joke was on them, and it made him feel more comfortable about himself. He smoked cigarettes and watched the orange tips get brighter and brighter as the sun went down. He looked at the girls coming in and out of the back door as they got ready for the dance. He did not drink, because he did not like the acrid taste of beer, yet he liked being here with them, knowing that every sip was what their own parents had done at their age. He did not mind seeing the others drunk—after a certain point, he knew that the drunker boys would sit next to him and talk. He would not respond except to smile, because he didn't know what else to do, what to make of their joking, their arms heavy around his shoulders.

They gathered themselves after the girls were ready and they walked to the hall, twos and threes along the sidewalk, some of them chewing big wads of hard pink gum and then spitting them into the grass. He was not as crass as the other boys, who waited to spit until they saw the dark figures of the churchgoers scowling from their porches. They divided mints between them when the hall came into view: the taillights of cars easing into the parking lot, women sitting in passenger seats waiting for their doors to be opened.

The boy got in line with the rest of them, watching as a pair of older women at the ticket table looked disapprovingly at the girls and motioned with their fingers for each of them to extend their arms. They fastened pink plastic bracelets around their wrists, ignoring the odor of alcohol. When the boy made it to them, he tried to move as close as possible, to show he was not like the rest of them, but one of the women only said, "No beer," strapping the pink bracelet tightly and taking his dollar bills.

Inside, his friends had already fractured. A flurry of kids their age milled around the edge of the dance floor while the older couples swayed gently to the band's ballad of horns and *bandeneón.* All he saw were bodies pressed together, light coming through in the spaces cleared for the dance steps of other couples, hips and fake jewelry catching. He saw the smoke blue in the air around the hanging lights;

the cigarettes, which he felt contributed to the heat; the men with unbuttoned shirt collars, their hands around the backs of laughing women.

When the song ended, with a long and mournful note on a single horn, the couples separated to applaud, and some of the women went back to their own tables. He saw that people of every situation were there—older, single women sitting at the circular tables, men his father's age with shiny belt buckles and boots. Of his own age, the boys were pestering some of the older men to buy them beer, hiding the telltale pink bands that showed their age, sneaking sips in the darker shadows of the hall's great room.

As the next song began—a wild, brash *ranchera* complete with accordion at full expansion—the milling began again, people alone, people together. He put his hands in his pockets while men removed their hats and cornered women for a dance. Couples with joined hands pushed their way to the floor that had only just settled its dust. Some alone, some together. The music roared its way through the hall, and the boy reasoned that everyone felt the way he did at the moment— lost and unnoticed, standing in place as he was.

The boy's mother spreads the concoction more vigorously, her son's legs giving way where the flesh is soft, reminding her that he is not fully grown, not a man yet. She believes her rubbing will wake him, and when he doesn't respond, she looks at her husband, who does nothing but look back.

She speaks to her son. "Are you awake?" she asks him, her hands grasping his legs quickly to shake him, but he only stirs, his head moving to one side and then stopping. "Are you in pain?"

Her husband stands up to look closely at their son's face and says to her, "His eyes are open." He waves his hand slowly in front of the boy, but still he will not speak. "I don't think he sees me."

"Are you awake?" she says again, rising to see for herself. His eyes are open, just as her husband said, but they don't seem to stare back at her. She thinks for a moment that his open eyes will begin to water and she waits for him to blink, but he only closes his eyes once more.

"It's early still," the father says. "Don't worry."

The boy felt as if he had been the only person to notice the man with the plain silver buckle, a belt that shimmered against the glow of the yellow bulbs strung across the hall's high rafters. A plain silver buckle that gleamed like a cold eye, open and watching. Even from a distance, the boy knew it was plain, that it had no etchings, no tarnish, no scratches. He watched it tilt at the waist as the man put his boot up on the leg of a stool, leaning down to one of the girls who had come with the boy, whispering to her.

He felt as if he were the only one watching how the girl flicked her hair deliberately with her left wrist, as if to show the pink bracelet in a polite gesture to move on: she was too young.

The boy pictured himself with the same kind of arrogance, the posture that cocked the man's hips, the offering he suggested to this girl, and he wondered if he would ever grow into that kind of superiority, being capable of seducing and tempting. He watched the silver buckle blink at him, as if it watched back, as if it knew where the boy was looking.

The man finally left the girl alone, but the boy watched him, circling the dance floor, sometimes losing him between songs as the hall dimmed the lighting to invite a slow dance. Or losing him when one of the other boys distracted him with a stolen beer. But he would quickly find him again, the belt buckle gleaming and catching—a circle of silver light moving through the dark tables.

The girl from before came up to the boy and said, "That man kept bugging me," as if she expected the boy to do something about it. He turned to look at her—she was one of the girls who regularly went to church, didn't know how to behave at a dance, put up her hair because her girlfriends told her to. And now, with that strange man, she wanted trouble for its own sake, he thought. He could hear in her voice that she wanted the attention in some form—his defense, or that man's proposal—so no one would look at her as the girl with the straight dark hair, a Sunday girl.

So the boy moved, without looking at the girl, keeping his eye on the silver buckle and followed the man, catching up to him toward the back of the hall, where only the couples who could not wait to get home were kissing, leaning against each other, backing into the wall. The man stood next to a woman, facing her and talking among all the bodies rubbing against each other, his silver buckle the only still thing, and the boy noticed that the man wore nothing but black, down to his boots. The man's teeth gleamed as he smiled, watching the boy approach. He smiled as if he expected him and ignored the woman, who disappeared into the dark bodies.

Before the boy could say anything about the girl, the man extended his hand, offering a beer. "My apologies," he said to the boy, his voice clear and strong, and the boy noticed his face—what a handsome man he was, his skin as dark as anyone's in town—but his voice not anchored by the heaviness of accent. He was not like them, the boy knew instantly.

The mother opens all the doors in the house, though the sky doesn't look as if it will break one way or the other. She draws more curtains, all the rooms filled with the muted daylight. Even the closet doors are open, flush against the walls, and she pushes the clothes apart to allow the light in the tight spaces. She thinks of the kitchen cabinets and the drawers, the small knobs that pull out of tables and nightstands, the blankets hiding the dust motes under the beds. The husband lets her do this and then says nothing as she sits in the living room all by herself with her head in her hands.

Because the front door is wide open, she hears the footsteps on the sidewalk long before they approach the house, and she looks to the porch to see a group of her son's friends coming. They walk so close together; they seem afraid and apologetic at the same time. All of them have their heads bowed, the girls and the boys in fresh Sunday church clothes, and she knows they see the mess her son made on the front lawn.

It is odd for her to be sitting on her living room couch and seeing not the television but her own front yard, and she can do nothing but watch as the boys and girls stop at the porch, almost startled that they do not have to knock.

"What do you want?" she hears her husband say, and she turns to see him in the archway to the kitchen, where he must have heard them coming. "What did you give him last night?"

Her husband's voice is filled with rage, but she can see that her son's friends have come out of concern. And she knows they will tell her that her son had not been drinking, that they will deny that he took any drugs, and she will believe them. But she knots her fingers and her hands, trying to build up a false anger, because she is too ashamed and afraid to let them know what she and her husband saw on her boy's body, the things he said in a voice that was not his, how the house seemed to swell and breathe as if it were living itself, the whole space filling out in the same terrible way that her chest wanted to burst forth.

"We didn't give him anything," one of the boys says. "He wouldn't even take one beer."

"He's sick now!" her husband yells at them. "You understand that? ¿Entienden?"

"Let them go home," the mother says. "They don't need to know anything."

The boys and girls still stand on the porch, because they see she has been talking to her husband and not them, waiting for him to order them away. But the husband does not say anything, and then one of the boys speaks up and says, "I brought him home because we found him sick. Outside the hall. He was just sick. We don't know how."

No one responds, no one asks questions. Not the husband, not the mother. And just when the mother is about to rise from the couch to point her finger to the street, to show them away from the porch, they all know to look in the hall archway leading to the bedroom. There, clad only in his underwear, his skin pale and the dampness of the day swimming through the house, stands the boy.

He is aware of himself in a way that is unsettling, as if he has escaped his body once and for all and yet, exhausted as he feels, knows that his body is his own again. He is aware that the window to his bedroom is open and the day is overcast; the curtains move in a breeze that is chilly and has made the sheets underneath him cold. He shivers.

He hears the voices in the front of the house, the sound of his father's anger, the way only his father can sound, and his mother's hesitations. He hears the sounds of his friends but can't tell how many.

He feels the cold on his legs and he rises from the bed slowly, putting his feet on the floor, and the act of moving—like water, like the leaves outside his bedroom window today—startles him, the ease of it. Looking at his thin legs, the hollow of his own chest, he does not feel ashamed of himself as he once did.

The boy knows what he has done, what has happened, and yet, deep inside, he believes it could not have been. He thinks back to the man in the black clothes and the silver buckle, the offered beer, and the few words they spoke. The man had asked him if he spoke Spanish and when he had said no, the man had looked almost pleased. He does not remember what else they might have spoken of, only that the hall seemed to tilt and sway, the *ranchera* amplified to ten times as loud as he has ever heard, so that the man's voice came from within him. It came from the darkness when he closed his eyes to the hall's dipping and sinking, and when he opened them, it was still dark and he felt the nip of the outside air, the summer night cool compared to the pushed-together bodies of the dance inside. The cool of the sheets beneath him this morning makes him recall that outside air, how he had felt it not against his face but the bare skin of his chest, then his belly, and the metallic touch of the silver belt buckle pressing close.

The music was distant—they were away from the hall, away from the cars in the parking lot, where couples were leaving, the engines starting. He recalls now the rough edges of a tree against his back, the bark and the summer sap, the branches a canopy that hid the stars, because he looked up and saw nothing but the spaces between leaves, small stars peeking through to see him.

He had said nothing to this man, remembers how he allowed the man's hands to grab his waist, his entire arm wrapped around, lifting the boy's feet from the ground, the feeling of rising, almost levitating. He felt as if the man rose with him because he felt the hot press of the man's belly, the rough texture of hair, and now he remembers how he had let his hands run down the man's back, the knots on his spine, the fine-worked furrow, their feet on air. He kept looking up, searching for the stars between the branches.

The man, his back broad, grunted heavily. The sound frightens the boy now as he recalls it in broad daylight. The man's sound made him grow, pushing the boy up higher and higher, to where the boy could see himself in the arms of the man who glowed in the darkness of the canopy of branches, his skin a dull red, the pants and boots gone. And though he felt he was in air, he saw a flash of the man's feet entrenched fast in the ground—long, hard hooves digging into the soil, the height of horses when they charge—it was then that the boy remembers seeing and feeling at the same time—the hooves, then a piercing in the depth of his belly that made his eyes flash a whole battalion of stars, shooting and brilliant, more and more of them, until he had no choice but to scream out.

And now, at midmorning, his father and mother in the front of the house, his skin smelling of mint and roses, he knows enough to go forward and send his friends away. He wonders if he will sound different; he wonders if they will see how he carries himself now; he remembers how feeling the furrow of the man's back reminded him of the hard work of picking grapes in the summer months—his father will punish him with it. The hard work and the rattlers under the vines, their forked tongues brushing the air, and the boy remembers that the man's tongue pushed into his with the same vigor, searching him with the same kind of terrible flick.

He rises from the bed and steps, with an unfamiliar grace, to the wide-open door of his bedroom and down the hall.

The mother sees him, the look in his eye, and she wants to say nothing at all. She believes, as she always has, that talking aloud brings moments to light, and she has refused to speak of her mother's death, of her husband's cheating, of the hatred of her brothers and sisters. She sees her son at the doorway and wants to tell him not to speak.

They all stand and wait for the boy to talk, the doors and windows open as wide as possible and every last secret of their home ready to make an easy break to the outside. The curtains swell with a passing breeze.

"You're awake," the father says, and walks toward the boy, and the mother hopes that he will not speak and reveal his voice. She wonders if her husband knows now, if he can tell how the side-to-side swivel of the dancers at the hall and the zigzag of their steps have invited an ancient trouble, if her husband knows the countless stories of midnight goings-on, of women with broken blood vessels streaming underneath their skin from the touch of every strange man.

She keeps wondering, even when her husband turns to the boy's friends and tells them, "See? He's fine. Now go home," and motions them away from the porch and they leave without asking her son anything at all. She wonders now if her husband has ever awakened at night, dreaming of dances where bags of church-blessed rattlesnakes have been opened in the darkness of the place, the mad slithering between feet and the screams, the rightness of that punishment, the snakes that spoke in human voices, the rushed side-to-side movement of the snakes before they coiled underneath tables to strike at ankles.

When her husband turns his back to walk to the porch, watching the boy's friends walk off warily, she takes her chance and rushes to her underwear-clad son in the archway and grabs him by his arms—his flesh cold—and says, under her breath, "I know, I know," and then bravely, without waiting to hear what his voice might sound like, tries to pry open his mouth and check for herself.

The Third Myth

I

For a pregnant woman, any time the full moon is in cycle is cause for concern. Of course, if the woman steers clear of being outdoors at night without her husband, then the threat is much reduced. It is extremely dangerous, however, on the rare events that a lunar eclipse is predicted. With her husband's help, a woman should pierce her belly button with a clean safety pin, firmly clasped. Or, if this is too painful, simply latched to the woman's blouse where the cloth touches the navel. White cotton is best.

II

Pochi didn't turn out right. Not many of us did, according to my mother, or her friend Doña Rosita. Probably, if you asked Pochi's mother herself, she would say the same, she would say so.

If I didn't come to be right, it's because of Drino—Sandrino—Velásquez, who plays basketball as a starter and drives a Chevy Vega that his brother fixed up for him, chrome rims so bright and polished they look like diamonds when he drives to pick me up three blocks away from home, where my mother can't see from the window.

Because of me, I think Drino's mother would say that he didn't turn out right, either. She would say to my mother, It's your son's fault.

And because after basketball practice, I don't go home but wait for

Drino outside the locker room when I'm done. The other guys come out one by one with bags, sweatshirts draped over their bare shoulders. Drino is not last, and we walk together to his car and drive to the back parking lot, which is nearly empty.

Drino turned out right this way: he is lean, and even though his legs are skinny, I can feel how running on the court has made them hard above the knee, inside the thigh when I run my hand up the shorts of his uniform. It is that kind of moment, and he is saying things to me as his hands move across, as he moves himself on top of me. I can feel the bones in his back waiting to widen and imagine how much more of a man than me he will become, soon.

It is cold, even for April in this town, where basketball is all year, and the darkness behind the gym makes the night colder, since the seats are not cloth but vinyl. I pull Drino close, and then closer, his shorts gathered at his knees. He's taken off his jersey, only the gold chain tight around his neck. It's how his mother wants him to be, to keep him good. But the tiny cross means something else whenever I see it rest where it does, where it can't move, because his shoulders— the small muscles in his neck—are growing, and that necklace is from too many Christmases ago.

If my mother saw this, she would be asking why I am letting this happen. She would say that it is Drino who is doing this to me; I can change. Drino has looped a cross around his rearview mirror to remind him. Drino grips, harder, and we make the wooden cross on the mirror sway, back and forth, No. No.

This is my failure, is Drino's as well, about how we didn't learn to take, about how neither of us turned out right. But I don't want to think we are wrong, because all of our friends have done the same— maybe not this—but they try to pretend they are still good.

Then there's Pochi, who isn't a friend, has other things to worry about, is different in how he is not right.

Through the window, fogged because it's cold out, he has moved so quietly to peer closer at us. And when I gasp, "Drino!" it is to get Drino to see him, and Drino turns and yells, "You fuck!" Drino's back turns rigid in my hands as he fumbles for the door handle. "You fuck!" he yells again. "You fucker!" and the door opens, Drino spilling out. I catch a glimpse of Pochi trying to stuff himself back into his pants. The night air comes in crisp and sharp and I pull on the sweatshirt Drino never wore. Drino is still yelling, his skinny back bare, his ass naked, and I think of how it, too, is going to become hard. And beyond him is Pochi, ill-formed form, his running a hunched gallop, his arms and shoulders not able to work the way they should, half running, half grappling with his pants.

Even with our wrongs, he is not like us: I can hear him against Drino's barking voice. Pochi's reply is a twisted huff that must travel through a body that is not straight. And when his voice hits the clear cold air, it speaks like a note from a crumpled trumpet, a sound harsh in its greed to leave its frame.

III

Doña Rosita sells lipstick, powders to make the cheeks red in small circles, pencils, brushes, and creams. She has twin daughters who come along with her (and are quiet in the living room) every time she visits my mother. The girls are eight and they wear wide skirts, white and thick clothed that cover the lips of their knees.

My mother and her, they talk and drink coffee, and Doña Rosita has my mother close her eyes to apply a new shade of shadow, and they do all of this in the kitchen, where nothing is simmering.

It is mid-April and Easter has come and gone. And with it Lent, and now my mother has gone back to what she refused, all those days of going to church with a pale, somber face. "Because this is a time to remember his sacrifice," my mother had told us, and promptly ordered us to give up the valuable. For me, going out on the weekends; and for my father, watching television. My brother, who's older and in his last year of high school, said he'd give up going out, too, but he would disappear on Friday afternoons for the entire weekend and my mother would never say a word.

"You should try some of this new eye shadow," Doña Rosita says, but she does so in a quiet voice, casting a quick eye to her girls in the living room.

"Not too dark, but not bright, either," my mother tells her, her eyes still closed and jittery as she anticipates Doña's fingers.

I'm standing near the stove, not wanting to sit down, Doña's makeup sample case open and brilliant in its dark hues. Out in the living room, the TV is on, but I know Doña had long since taken the liberty to change the station away from *telenovelas* or cartoons or even the English-language soaps, so the girls are probably watching a cooking show. I lean over and pick up a dark orange lipstick.

"Put that down," my mother says, though her eyes still look closed. "Don't be rude."

"Go ahead," says Doña. "I don't mind."

"Kids," my mother says. "Manners."

"True," says Doña with her twin daughters, still painting my mother's right eyelid, and then shows her with a mirror, "Look."

"Oh," my mother says, moving her face this way and that, "I like it," and then turns to the little case holding the eye shadow. "Let's do this one," she points, and Doña takes a small towel wipe between her fingers and has my mother close her eyes again.

"True, true," says Doña, going back to work, "all of that true. My girls, I make them behave, but it's easy, because I only need to do one, and the other one copies her."

"Better early," my mother says. "I tell my two boys to be careful and watch out. Look at La Victoria. You see?" my mother says, and now the conversation sounds like it is not just between them, because she seems to be looking at me through her closed eyes.

"I always told La Victoria that it wasn't good to wear so much," says Doña. "But I never want to tell other people how to be, right?

So I told her that it could make her face get wrinkles too fast, or that it would sag, but she just overdid it, trying to get that man."

"Well, she got him."

"*Pobrecita,*" Doña says, "even if she asked for it. Look at what she has to live with now, with that son of hers. *Que Dios lo bendiga a él tambien,*" she says, and I wonder if she really means it, if she really wishes God to bless Pochi. For what? To make him not what he is? To help him when he passes away from this world?

"You see what can happen?" my mother tells me again, her eyes shut, Doña's squinting as she applies even more carefully, and they both look like they're ready to predict doom for me through their tight eyes, that they foresee someone like Pochi as a consequence for not listening.

"*Ay,* my twins," Doña Rosita says, as if in anticipation.

"Poor thing," says my mother.

IV

Pochi's name is not really Pochi, not in that hospital room where they keep records that have a footprint and the signature of the doctor who delivered every baby in this town. His name is Francisco, and I remember his mother called him Pancho when he was little, when we knew (even then) that something was not going to be right with him, that he would not catch up with us as we ran up and down the street. He sat in his dirt yard and drew circles around himself, more and more of them, and spit, grumbling. And then his mother would yell for him from the front porch. It would take him some time before he realized he was being called, and he'd get up on all fours and scamper to the front door.

To be mean, someone called him Puchi—which is what we would say when we crinkled our noses on Gold Street where the sewer always leaked up onto the pavement and where the Martinez family lived with their new set of triplets and an overflowing can of diapers. But Pochi didn't smell at all. I remember Mrs. Patterson asking me to help him with his fractions back in the seventh grade, and he smelled like purple flowers, like the lilac on the bottle of perfume that my mother ordered from the TV.

He's been kept with us, even though we're sophomores now and I know he can't read. Pochi faces the wall in the cafeteria because someone yelled at him for chewing gross, because Pochi has no teeth on his bottom jaw and he tilts his head to chew a hamburger, like a cat. He's gotten pudgy now, especially in the legs, and his head looks like it's stopped growing. Nothing's right for him.

The only time I ever see him outside of school is at the football games in the autumn, the harvest moon out and Pochi's hunched form in the corner of the bleachers. He's the team's biggest supporter, jumps up at even the bad plays, and he yells with that voice that seems so glad to escape into the air, and those are the times that I know something occupies him, that he can watch the guys on the field completely hidden by helmets and padding and uniforms—made bigger, wider, fleet—and he knows there's something to hitting a person with that force. He shrieks when someone gets hurt, even if it's the home team, and everyone in the stands turns to look at him and snicker. But they know him and see that it's okay.

In the cafeteria, every day, I see the back of his head. Pochi's hair is black, thick, and cut short all around. I know his mother must have shaved his face for him because his hands are not steady. His cheeks and chin are always shady and ready to sprout. I've never been close enough to look in his eyes.

I've never wanted to look into his eyes.

His mother, La Victoria, is a beautiful woman, if she weren't so angry. I don't know why Pochi didn't turn out like her or his father. I've heard his father was a beautiful man.

V

"Drino," I ask on another night, parked much farther from the gym, keeping a lookout for cars, "do you think you'll get punished for any of this?"

"What?" he asks. Tonight he didn't let me touch him and he came dressed in the sweatshirt, the night foggy for so late in April, and it is safe to park. "You mean by my mom, or what?"

"No," I say, "I mean later. When we grow older."

"Like how?" he asks. The fog is cold, makes the car cold, and I want to slide closer next to him, but I stay on my side and peer around, the back parking lot empty as usual.

"Bad things," I tell him. "Bad things happening to us."

"What are you talking about?" Drino turns to me and he reaches for the pack of cigarettes resting on his dashboard. He takes one out to twirl it in his fingers. He does not smoke, only keeps the pack there opened, in case anyone ever came around and then he could say we had just been smoking.

"It was only a couple of times. And once for real. No big deal. What? Do you think something's going to happen to you?" His voice rises when he asks me and I want to tell him that yes, maybe something will. To me. And that for him, his back might not widen, that he might remain small, and his body might become not-right.

"You're full of shit," he tells me. And then, "But we probably shouldn't be doing this kind of thing anymore."

VI

A young girl must arrive at her fifteenth year pure and churched. And if this is done, a father must celebrate the arrival, the devotion to purity, and the last half of the road to marriage. He must spare no expense in celebration, of calling upon the church for the ceremony, of alerting the neighbors that the day has come in all glory. A girl in white, standing at the brink of womanhood, close to God, is the first part of a lifelong blessing: children will be born, and these children will come into this world healthy, devoted to church and kindhearted, a wonderful reward for the devotion of such a girl, amid all the world's temptations and sinful behaviors.

Girls who are not pure should not attempt to deceive by wearing white

and gathering to celebrate. Nothing will befall them but misfortune: bad be-
havior is paid fivefold, through their children.

VII

My mother did not allow Doña Rosita into the house today, though her face needed the rosy polishes and the creams and powders. "Tell her to come back on Wednesday," my mother sobs at the kitchen table, and I whisper it to Doña Rosita and her twin daughters with the crossed arms.

My father is not home and I cannot tell what he will say when he hears that my brother has gotten his girlfriend pregnant. I cannot tell, from the way my mother is carrying on and looking at the ceiling, if he'll search my brother out with the back of his leather belt and demand an explanation. We've been told about all of this before, that there would be hell to pay.

"*Ay,*" my mother cries into her hands.

"Do you want some coffee?" I ask her, because I'm in the kitchen and don't know what to do.

She nods at me and sniffles. "She's so young, that girl."

With my back to her, I fill the pot and try to figure out what to say. When me and Drino have complained about this town, how there's nothing for us here, I can say for myself (though not for him) that I've thought about chance, how it happened that I was born in this tiny place in that hospital with that doctor. Of all places. And now my brother and that girl, they'll be bringing in a new one to this town. I don't know how to say, but I try. "Things will be all right, I guess. You'll see."

"Ricardo." She says my name, over and over again. She is sobbing, and through it I expect to hear my brother's name, but she only repeats mine. As the coffeepot gurgles, she tells me, "*Que Dios te bendiga. That you don't do this to us, m'ijo.*"

I remain in the kitchen with her and say nothing. I cannot look at her. And when the coffee is ready, I stir in sugar and enough milk to make it almost cool, so she can sip it right away, so we can stay quiet.

VIII

The late evening comes in a flurry, the April evening, and with it the same cold. My father comes through the house like a bad cloud because he already knows, my mother having called him at the auto garage. My brother has made the mistake of being home.

My father is a man whose arms are on the verge of splitting from so much work, of lifting tires and twisting bolts that won't give for anyone else. Tonight, he didn't bother to take off his boots at the front door, went immediately to our bedroom door and pounded it open, unstrapping his belt.

I am still in the kitchen with my mother and neither of us moves. I don't want to see them go at it, though I can hear my big brother curse at our father every time the buckle bruises into him, the two of them slamming into my brother's dresser and my soccer trophies. And when my brother runs from the room and darts out of the front door, the screen door breaking from its hinge, I know he'll be back tomorrow to get his things and money from my mother.

My father emerges from the broken room and walks into the kitchen. To me, with belt still in hand, he says, "You . . ." accusingly, but says no more. Just us in the kitchen, my mother sitting, my father with belt in hand, and me not sure what to do, not able to imagine how he would use the belt if I completed his sentence, if I could get the words out of my mouth before the first blow.

IX

For many days our house is solemn, and the absence of my brother and his many things only reassures me that he will be back, begging, because life is hard, and the young girl will be in tow. It has always worked like that in our town, with all our friends, because girls are always the ones who cause the most disappointment, are never let back in. They have to find forgiveness somewhere else, with a boy's mother who decides to help in the end.

But until then, even my father goes to church with us, and I kneel beside my mother and must show her that I use beads with true faith, and I know my father is watching me now. Late April is broadening into evenings that are much shorter, and it's just as well—the spot behind the gym will no longer be dark until much later, until way after practice. We would go to the orchards now if I could go out with Drino, but every night keeps me in with my father, who is not drinking with the men after work anymore. Only at home, as if he's keeping guard.

Finally, in early May, when my brother comes with pregnant girl in hand, my father listens while drinking a beer. And when they all sit around the kitchen table to talk about money and work and school, that's when I slip out.

X

The test for willful boys, for stubborn ones, is the baked pie that is not for consumption, made from: flour, water, baking powder, lard, salt, a filling of uncooked pork. The child's hand should be pressed into the pie's raw top crust and the pie baked, and the oven not opened for one hour.

It should be cause for prayer if the handprint becomes misshapen in the course of baking. The hand of a good son will remain straight in indentation, evenly brown in the dips of each finger. A ruined crust spells trouble and serves as a warning to both parent and child. This should be done at a young age—six to eight is recommended—since, at times, the handprint will shape itself into a claw or hoof. This should not frighten anyone but should be shown to the child as a warning that bad behavior will bring this deformation as punishment. Parents, if they are truly devoted to church, will not fear it as the devil's announcement but as a heavenly sign and will be assured that the son will not try them.

XI

Drino arrives in his car and we drive out to the orchards, his cigarette pack on the dashboard, and out there we park, where the town lights are dim and far away and the peach trees make the night darker.

We don't speak, though I want to tell him how frightened I am. Tonight he is not hesitant; it has been a while. He crowds into me so forcefully that my face is pressed into his neck, into the small gold loops of his necklace.

Because of him and what we begin to do, I worry. I think of my brother and his girlfriend, what they are paying for, and how. I am afraid that if I look out the car window, we will be seen.

I think of Pochi being in the orchard, him being sent to look at me in warning, but I have decided that someone like him is not placed on this earth as a punishment for someone else. He is more than reminder. I feel sorry for him facing the wall, as much as I feel frightened for myself.

I look at the tiny cross that rests around Drino's neck and worry and fear what I might be made of. What is in me and how it gets out.

Drino says nothing, just moves his hands, our skin, and the orchard keeps getting darker on this off road. The peach orchards have already bloomed full, pink flowers by this time of year, but they crowd themselves into night nonetheless. Something will emerge from them to catch me. A pair of eyes looking, coming.

Tiburón

The man who sells shark teeth has made it to our town finally. We've been hearing about him for some time now and it was through the south side of town that he decided to come, pushing his wooden wheelbarrow in front of him, the necklaces. If you'd been here yesterday or the day before that (any day but today, before you got used to the town scent), you would have said apricot, something fruity, the heaviness of sawdust, of cherry wood. You would not have said salt, or cannery oil hanging heavy, seagull feathers. You would have known that waiting for this man was going to take a long time, because we're far away from waves. This is a town to wonder in, about that man and why he's bringing shark teeth, all the way out here.

Chela tells us that cows have the same kind of teeth. That the necklaces are from their open mouths, the cows having dehydrated in the foothills this past summer and the farmers thought it too difficult to get to their hillside carcasses, in the yellow grass and the rattlesnakes. She has seen this man picking at the rotting heads of the cows, that he carried pliers and a little saw. His wooden wheelbarrow at the side of the road and him shouting at the birds to get away.

He comes now, down our street, without bells or horns like the men selling snow cones from their three-wheeled bicycles. We came out because we've been waiting and thought we could hear the clatter of the necklaces against each other, all the way down the street, though they're not hanging but coiled one on top of the other. In the dust of the road, we wait barefoot, and he's in no hurry.

In a little brown cloth sack held in the palm of his hand, he accepts our dimes and quarters and then, around each of us, he ties a tooth. Each on a brown leathery string that, after he's gone, will leave our necks stained with a sticky oil. No, you can't have two, he tells us, just one, and it's not a toy. And to show us, he takes a face, the left cheek in his old hand, and with his other hand he traces an X on the right cheek with the sharp tip of tooth. The lines begin, but do not bleed, do not break.

"*No es juguete, niños,*" he tells us again.

We don't believe Chela anymore, but we do listen to Pancha, and she says she knows why the man comes. Because he is like the spiders that we step on, the daddy longlegs that crawl down from the corners of our houses, that you must throw them out after you hear them pop. If not, their little babies come in the middle of the night to slip up your nose, in your mouth and ears to lay more eggs and turn your body into a web.

And this tooth?

This tooth is simple—we can't take it off now. We must search for it in the morning when we open our eyes, and if it isn't there, then we know it has gathered with the other teeth around the neck of a child who doesn't wear one. It has gathered with its brothers and sisters to ring tight and push through a sleeping neck till the skin breaks. We're glad that the man came today, because we've been hearing too much about him in the school yard, the boys kicking dust and saying that it isn't true, but they are like us and stay awake at night. In the dark, awake, even if brothers are there and snoring.

And even now, the dust-kicking boys do the same we do. They cannot sleep. They hold their shark tooth between their fingers and poke themselves with it if their eyes shut, won't let it leave now that they have it. Never wanted it to come in the first place.

Museo de Bellas Artes

The museum opens today, says the newspaper, the headlines in special color print. It will be free this week, after the ribbon snip. But we do not believe it will happen, even when the town beauty queen officially raises the scissors in a welcome gesture.

We have a right to be suspicious. Too much time has passed since the town grandly embraced a rich farmer from the South Valley, handshakes on the front page of the *Herald,* the announcements that our town would elevate itself from the ones around it through history.

We have waited through two springtimes, watched the museum sitting on risers and concrete blocks after the move from its old spot on our side of town, next to the railroad tracks. Before, it housed an A&W and its roller-skating girls. But they've restored the maple-framed train schedules and the placards when the museum had been a depot, a stop for women on their way north with umbrellas and gifts of almonds and figs, the men who accompanied them, how they wore pants that were thin striped and perfectly tailored.

Today, they undraped the mural of James S——, our town founder, so that he will preside over the front entrance. He is a man of enormous eyes. The portrait shows him seated, his legs giant flanks, a gold watch painted so brilliantly in its loop that we doubt the sun will ever fade it. He appears pleased with everyone wanting to enter his museum.

We think it is a pretty building now and wish it had been so when it was on our side of town. It had suffered a blistered coat of sulfurous yellow and a brown trim. Today it is a fresh petal-blue, and the town employed bricklayers to position a walkway in its new yard, one that splits to circle around a tiny electric fountain. For weeks, they have turned on the orange lights in the bottom of the fountain's pool, and the reflected droplets come down as if on fire. We came to see it at night and left, excited.

But it has been so long that we don't know what to expect once the beauty queen lets us in. The baby palms they planted have grown full frond; they are shoulder height to us now, and the tops of them clip past the thin iron gates. Luckily, it is morning and the sun is not difficult, and we wait patiently in the line, the beauty queen greeting everyone as they trickle inside.

Modesto, a stupid boy we know, has been through it and exits, tells us that the museum is no good and the people in front of us shoot him looks for speaking ill of it. He claims it is nothing but unharnessed plows, purple with rust, farm equipment that was never owned by anyone famous, politician or gangster.

We prepare to be disappointed. Some of us hope that we might see a beautiful painting, or a marble sculpture like the ones in our social studies books. Or old guns, the bullets taken from a fallen bandit or a murdered mayor.

But with all the pushing and shoving, there is no time to see into the glass casings or read the print. We glimpse a hoopskirt and the trampled black shoes of a woman with minuscule feet. A town map superimposed over James S———, a letter tacked to the side with his request for numerical streets. Our town never got that big. Second Street. Then pockets of order: streets for colleges (Harvard, Yale, Princeton); counties bordering ours (Inyo, Kern); lusty Spanish (Amador).

We came away empty, no photographs, nothing to hold, the gift shop packed with people and expensive, and on our way out, we knew that we would not step in again. Not for the five dollars after this opening week. And what if beautiful things came there to be shown, as the town began promising? Opulent masks from Mexico, arrowheads, and green feathers. Where would we be, not able to see them, as they sat inside the new building, so freshly blue?

I will admit to you that I touched the fringe of a yellowed gown on display when the others were not looking. A woman behind me slapped my hand and told me not to do it again, that it was a delicate thing and my fingers could damage it. But when we all left, I rubbed my fingers together and the softness came again, how the gown would retain what I gave it.

The Unimportant Lila Parr

Lila Parr is the white woman, their neighbor, and a young widow. She is the one who reminds the man of the days when he worked the acres that he now owns. The man has inherited these acres, the land given to him by Lila Parr's husband. Lila Parr is now forty and still wears the dresses she did when she brought out trays of biscuits and lemonade for the workers. The man remembers what she looked like even then. She was only twenty and newly married. All of her dresses had the deep color of their cotton dyes. She held trays with both hands and smiled at the workers. It is Lila Parr's kindness that the man remembers, how she treated the men who could not speak English to her.

And he believes it is Lila Parr's kindness that has allowed him to own the small farm and its toolshed, several acres of orchards on all sides. The townspeople always said that Lila's husband was a good person. But even the man cannot imagine how her husband would have been able to name beneficiaries on his last days. Because the man witnessed how quickly the trembling of the old Parr barn became a crash and how the rafters and the spray of dust and splinters brought Lila's husband to one knee. For a moment, her husband balanced on one knee before the full weight of the building came down and silenced even his groans; he never said another word. With rising dust all around them, the man and the other workers shouted to him, "¡Señor! ¡Señor Parr!" but their panic could do nothing to slow the damage inside, the fluid collecting in the young man's lungs.

Lila Parr lives in a small house just down the road, but still close. It is one that was built especially for her after her husband's death, because she wanted to remain close to the land he tilled. In the evening, the man can see her little house and its windows glowing through the night because she is alone and has remained childless after all these years. He has always felt for her loneliness.

The man and his wife have done with little breakfast. Usually, she will set out a plate of eggs, chorizo or bacon, ham, oatmeal, and coffee. She will advise him to eat fruit, and he will complain that he deals with fruit all day, but she is insistent. But today, he made do with toast and coffee because she had not gone out to get groceries. She did not want to drive the miles into town.

This morning, she stood by the stove as if it were a foggy winter day and not late August. It is during the winter that she struggles the most to wake in the dark of four-thirty. She will huddle with him in December because the rest of the house is chilly, all four burners on, breakfast frying. Now, in August, she watched only a lukewarm coffeepot and said little to him. She has been awake since two in the morning, the knock at the door, two officers telling them about their son found dead. She has sobbed but not spoken. But she did, this morning, open her mouth to mention Lila Parr. She told him that Lila Parr offered to make the trek into town, that she will be the one to bring back eggs and pork chops and bread.

All morning, the man has been thinking of answers. Only today has he considered the work in the farm office taxing; he has rarely ever looked up from his desk in the old, converted shed to see the full fields. There has always been activity: workers picking the peaches, loading crates, reminders of when he did that kind of labor, how he cannot do so now even when the weather threatens or a final shipment of fruit will be the only money for the month. His days have always been shuffling—invoices for farm equipment; legal documents challenging land distribution and his English; orders for seed and sod.

The man is so heavily troubled that he has taken to raking the leaves beneath the stunted peach trees outside the shed office. There are a few leaves on the ground, yellow and golden in the dust. It is late August, the peaches only recently picked, not time for the leaves to begin turning such colors. The trees give worthless peaches. He rakes underneath until thin spokes are left in the dust, and he notes how the peach trees have been arching their roots above the hard soil. They will need to be pulled soon; he thinks he should have done so already, as if the trees suffer physically for lack of water, a dull pain in the leaves.

It was Lila Parr who helped his only son plant the stunted peach trees over twenty years ago. Lila gave the boy a red water pail, and he nurtured the seedlings as best he could. She walked behind him as his son struggled to carry the red pail with both tiny hands. When the seasons turned, the man and his wife admired the budding leaves and the blossoms as the trees grew. They watched Lila Parr get on the ground with their son and weed the patch in front of the farm office. Her cotton dresses with the deep dyes had worn circles at the elbows, the hems beginning to unravel. Even before they thanked her, Lila told them how important it was for her to be with their son, that she would care for the boy whenever they needed to attend the county fair or the auctions. She continued with her hands in the soil, until both her thumbs and the boy's rawed at the tips.

That evening, the man stands outside of his small farmhouse, and he sees the lights of Lila Parr's windows shine against the approaching darkness. Along the horizon, the dots of headlights make their way along Highway 99, red and white moving north and south. It is their sheer numbers that makes them noticeable. Any growing thing in the Valley could demonstrate vibrancy, but it is the lights that intrigue him most, because it signals that people are moving. They might be responding to a beckoning or running away from a trouble.

When the evening settles into night, Lila's windows glow. Night brings greater clarity; even through the trees, he sees the steady yellow dots of homes in all directions. Houses that are several miles away are still visible, their telltale lights pushing through all that distance.

He picks a dot along the strand of horizon lights and wonders if this might be the roadside motel just before the highway on-ramp. Its neon sign might be the blend of pink and amber that is shimmering in the distance. The motel is twelve rooms facing away from the glare and noise of the highway, its driveway dark. It is never more than half full.

The man wishes and then does not wish he had been standing here late last night, when he might have confirmed the motel location not only by its vague pink-and-amber glow but by a distant bathing of police colors. It is in one of these rooms that the man's son was found. It was this morning that the police informed them of what had happened—the vulgarity of it—and this is why Lila Parr offered to drive to town to do their errands, why the man has been absentminded all day. He has been listless and light-headed.

The man's wife always liked to go into town and spend more time than she needed to. While there has never been much variety in the downtown area, she has made sure to walk to each shop, rarely buying anything but always looking at items which hardly sold, like locally made glassware. There is one she loves—a long, thin vase that is so blue—the ridiculous price swirled in cursive on a tiny placard. It has been available for over a year. She recognizes that even her good fortune over the past years has never meant this kind of indulgence. But when she does buy items, she deliberately purchases ones that cannot be wrapped or put in a paper bag. About once a month, she's walked out of the flower shop with a large basket of daisies. Or she's purchased homemade soaps that smell like oatmeal-honey and lavender, with triple-looped lace as a handle.

The man's wife drives a fairly new car, and she knows that she's been in this town long enough for people to remember how she came into her prosperity. She knows they recognize her car as the Parrs' second-best. She sits rigid against her car seat when she drives, both hands on the steering wheel. Staring ahead, she pretends not to notice people, only bothering to wave at those who greet her first when they step into the crosswalk. She recognizes the change in herself— she doesn't look people in the eye anymore, only at their hands, what they take, what they give back.

The man thinks his wife is given to melodrama, of assigning meaning to useless things. She has saved their son's baby teeth and first shoes. In the kitchen, she keeps a drawer full of first-grade paintings and scribblings. Though she's given most of his childhood clothing to her sisters for their own babies, she has stored little pantsuits and shirts in boxes. The man walked into the house one day to see his wife and son sifting through these old clothes and laughing.

In boxes kept in a hall closet, she holds a stack of address books from their life back in Texas. Old electricity bill receipts that printed their former residences at a work camp. There are leather-bound books with tiny calendars from too many years ago. Given hard weather, the man believes his wife could never continue without these objects. The Valley is good in how it spares them this particular kind of agony; she could never bear a flood or terrible winds because of this weakness.

It is the next day and the man considers staying in bed, but the call for fruit shipments will overcome him if he allows the situation to get the upper hand. His wife stays in bed, though he knows Lila Parr has stocked their cupboards and their refrigerator. The man's wife turns over in the bed, and she nods halfheartedly when he asks if she would like coffee.

He cooks a full breakfast for both of them, leaving a plate for his wife on the stove, but she does not come into the kitchen by the time he makes his way outside to the shed office. He is not surprised that none of the workers came today, that they have allowed him this time of grief without being prompted.

Diligent, the man does as much paperwork as possible before he is forced to make phone calls. His voice unsteadies when he tries to put forth his questions. On the other end of the line, he imagines that questions are being withheld. By the fourth call, the quiver is gone, but the voices speaking to him still harbor a strangely reserved sympathy. He begins to wish that it had not been a roadside motel room, but a car accident, a negligent diesel truck, something that would remove the responsibility on his son's part.

Toward midmorning, he glances up from his desk and sees his wife balanced on the top step leading out from the kitchen door, Lila Parr in the backyard. His wife, even from here, appears unresponsive, her arms folded. Lila Parr is nodding her head and her lips move, and the man knows from her movements that she is the one who has coped with loss before. She was always too beautiful to have been childless. He looks at his own wife, how she stands on the brink of something, and can see her anger begin to light from across the yard, how much she is beginning to resent being like Lila Parr, suddenly childless.

In a local bakery, there are two old men who gather to have coffee and Mexican bread at five-thirty every morning. Two women own the shop, and they serve them their daily orders and then take turns kneading dough for the noon deadlines. The door to the shop will open, bells, and someone will come in to buy tea or doughnuts but never stay long at this hour. The two men greet everyone who walks in the door.

The men and the women know already about the discovery of the body in the roadside motel, even though the paper has yet to confirm it. Everyone who has walked into the shop has stopped long enough to discuss it with them, shaking their heads as they depart to work in another town.

Today, the women say they haven't seen the man's wife in town, not in the afternoons, not in the grocery store. One of the old men says that this is not surprising, that she must be humiliated by the ordeal. He reminds them of her posture, how she walks in town, or how her hands clutch at things with authority. It is because she knows what it is like not to have had things. The other old man says he remembers even now how she had struggled, trailing two handcarts behind her, one full of groceries only the employers ate, the other with sacks of beans and potatoes. For years, she brought things to others, came back the following day, always in a borrowed car. The women say that her demeanor is not different from those who've been as lucky, that there comes a haughtiness when the easy life is given and not earned. One of the women says that the man's wife seems pained to remember hard work, that even her life now is still too little payment for what she has had to live through. The way she stands, walks, looks past—it tells how she feels she deserves more. More of what is anyone's guess.

The man and his wife had been asked by the county sheriff to confirm at the coroner's office. She was reluctant to go with him but said nothing when he held open the front door, his car keys clutched in one hand. They drove the miles into town without saying much of anything to each other. It was dawn, only hours after their son had been found, both of them wide awake.

He was surprised by the efficiency of the place, the compassion evident in the quiet footsteps of the staff, the gentleness with which they answered the phones. For some odd reason, he had expected families sitting in huddles as they did at hospitals, but the coroner's was a sparse place.

Their son's body was naked and discolored, his eyes closed. His wife looked away and cried, but the man did not. He stared intently at his son's form, holding back questions. The sheriff had told him, though it had not been confirmed, that their son may have been strangled, that two needles had been resting on the nightstand. The man was embarrassed to ask the coroner if anything more had been determined. He knew that the culprit had been caught, down south in Bakersfield, a young man the same age as their son. He knew that their son's body had been found naked and he stopped himself from completing the picture with that young man's involvement. Still, before the coroner moved them back to the front office, the man looked at the blue-black of his son's penis, his nakedness, and his thin brown legs. He thought of the roadside motel, those rooms facing away from the road.

The townspeople, the vendors, the more distant neighbors—all of them broke their silences when the town paper ran the story. It printed not only the particulars—the time of day, the needles found, the fugitive captured—but also the mildest of the allegations, what the interviewed police stressed as "possible motives."

The man has had no choice but to field their sympathies, even as these people do so only to question him about his son. He is not sure at times if they mean well. He knows some of the members of the Iglesia de San Pedro and they have conferred with him, driving out to the farmhouse and asking him to reconsider his position in the world. When they left, he was angry for being so cordial with them.

The workers have returned with hushed respect, and they have picked several sections of the orchards in such quick time that they go home early. The man tells their foreman that he will pay them extra because of the missed days, and in response the foreman gives him a perplexed look.

Suddenly, the last days of August have slowed for him, and September proves late to arrive. The man considers how another crop rotation is rising in the schedule, and the work and wear of it weighs him too heavily. He knows if the farming cycle does not continue, the fields will have trouble regenerating, the constant attention that they need.

At times, he pays too much attention to the stunted peach trees and the leaves that have rapidly fallen from the branches. He kicks his boot into the roots poking through the dry soil, thinking their fate is appropriate. He has the silly urge to pull the trees out bare-handed but calms himself, the failed trees being too simple, because his son planted them and nurtured them with the red water pail. The man looks at how vainly the branches stretch into the sky, as if they've known for so many seasons that their time would come. But it is not due to his son, or because he cared for them.

All around him, the man knows, are signs of misfortune, of good and bad luck. It is the nature of fields and orchards. There have been whole crop failures, tiny worms in the young plums. The porch of their farmhouse has been sagging for years, he knows. The space where the Parr barn collapsed is a small grape vineyard, but its grapes are good for neither raisins nor wine. He does not blame the incident for this lack. It is just so.

Yet, even with this understanding, his heart sinks when he sees Lila Parr approaching from her small house. He can see her form making its way, knows she will come directly to him this time. The man has not spoken to her face-to-face since the discovery. He is ashamed.

She comes closer and closer, inevitable. She is coming to tell him about her own belief in retribution. She believes in misdeeds, though the man will want to tell her that no misfortune has run through her own body. It has been her husband. It has been his son. Past her, because it is still late afternoon, the lights in her house are not on, and when she returns after having spoken to him, she will have nothing to guide her along the dark path.

— —

There are twelve rooms in the roadside motel. Each one is identical, long rectangular rooms with wide back windows which open to the highway. There are thick drapes that block out the light and noise; they pull tight to the center of the curtain rods.

All rooms have only a single bed wide enough for two people, a nightstand with a lamp, a television mounted high on the wall. The televisions are old-fashioned ones, no remote controls, but free of scratches, the color and tint very sharp. A guest must decide what to watch and then reach up high to turn the dials. The motel owner receives written complaints in womanly writing, the flourished letters telling him how anyone small must move the armchair from the corner in order to reach the knobs.

The motel owner has chosen not to live in the town. There are people who come to spend a late evening in one of his rooms, and early on in his ownership, he had detested running into these people at the grocery store or the bakery shop. He's never refused, however, anyone's offer of extra money to help shield them.

The motel knows many people by face: he knows the town's ex-mayor, a beautician from Fresno, many truckers from Oregon and Washington State. He stated, to the police officer, that the young man they had found dead came in alone and, no, he had never seen him before. But he did not tell that he had seen a dark figure in the passenger seat of the young man's car: he allows people their dishonesties.

The motel owner knows the young man's father, though not by name, because of the resemblance, the rich, broad face. He recognizes the dark complexion and the height. The young man lacked the stance, but he seemed to be headed toward the same powerful build, his hands firm when he grasped the pen to sign in, the doorknob when he exited.

He knows the young man's father, knows the white woman he has brought, and knows, as well, that they do not live far away. The motel owner likes to concoct their reasons for coming these miles when they might have convenient, empty homes. But he knows the white woman's story, all about her husband. He has greeted the young man's father heartily every time, letting him know through his handshakes that there was no shame in the deal. He peeked through his office window in time to see the man lead the white woman to the farthest room, her right hand clutching her dress.

That man has not come around since. The motel owner has read the papers. He has denied that the motel allows such illicit activities, that he has never found such things as needles or plastic bags. He will wait to see what the young culprit caught in Bakersfield will say, but already the motel owner feels that the father will need comfort in understanding. He will consider writing to the young man's father and explaining that it was all about love as well as anger; he wants to write to him about his nightly vigil at the office window, witnessing people sneak away in secrecy, some for good reasons, some for bad. He will write and tell him, plainly, that he saw the young man step out of the car. Then the other young man and how they stood by the door, close together and tentative, and then rushed inside.

Swallow

You were a boy then. You are a boy now, because *boy* means a different thing. Look at those boys. Those boys looking at boys. But this is about way back when, as a little boy, and how you mimicked. You mimicked in the backyard the things you saw. They took you to the circus and you saw the strong man. You eyed the strong man at the circus the way only a boy can. You admired him.

And the man who swallowed the knife, he was the one you wanted to copy. You loosened a board from the back fence and crept up against the side of the house. Your shadow was against the house, dark and defined, and the board's shadow looked like the circus sword. It looked like it, but it wasn't. It wasn't that same impossible silver. It wasn't the glisten of the shaft, the face of the man who swallowed that knife, his teeth clicking against the edge. You thought you heard his teeth click, because everyone was so quiet.

You are no longer a boy. But you are one of those boys. And you behave like it's still a circus and everywhere below are triple nets waiting to catch you. You know cutthroats and maybe boys who want to cut your throat. You know boys who've swallowed fire. They ache for fire. It sits in their bellies and burns. You'll burn, your father tells you. You've burned already, for a strange boy who took you to a strange place. You did things that you no longer think are strange. He did not harm you in the way that boys like you are harmed. But still, you ache anyway. You ache like a boy with a slit throat, the slice clean and fine.

NO BLOOD

Campo

Just at the base of the foothills, the town levels a space for itself between the vineyards of summer raisins and the fruit orchards. Though some of the workers live in this town, it is mostly a place for wide, open-porched houses, white wood, painted just this past spring. The lawns look even greener because of the shade of Chinese elms, though most of the trees shed a dusty fungus from their leaves so that, by September, they'll have released too early. The streets run diagonal in places, the intersections in town meeting in curious six-way stops, small islands of parks dotting the gaps where the streets miss each other.

The women who live in these houses, while their men are away, spend their time browsing the downtown shops. Many like to visit the sewing-and-crafts store in particular, located on a choice corner of downtown and owned by a woman who lives in a bigger house than they do—she tends a porch that skirts all the way around the home, the floorboards painted gray, the rails flower lined. She sells them ribbon, fabric, picture frames handmade from nectarine wood. Because it is summer, she displays a long skirt that she made, modeled by the headless mannequin in her window. The women in town stop to admire the white, almost sheer cloth, the brilliant, delicately small orange poppies that pepper the fabric.

The workers, though, do not live close to downtown. Past the county courthouse, with its palm-lined lawn and arc of black gate, the main road continues and then blanches away to a crumbling, thinner passage. It travels past the gasoline tanks and the giant cooling sheds of the ice company. Past these structures, away from the sight of the rest of the town, is the workers' neighborhood. They can walk to town and often do, past the courthouse, past the window with the primped mannequin, to get groceries, about twenty minutes each way. Mostly, it is the wives who go, followed by shirtless children, and then return again. There is a park across the road from the county courthouse—the last, nicely kept park before the gasoline tanks and the ice company—and here, people stop if they are walking, to rest in the grass, just for a few minutes, because they carry perishables off both arms.

It was only at the beginning of summer that the labor camp—off an even more vague strip of road than the one that began to falter after the county courthouse—was started up again. Hidden from view of the road by a nest of nectarine trees, the changing light of early evening brought the first signs that the camp was back in operation. At the workers' park, when the grass cooled and people relaxed, ribbons of smoke rose from the direction of the camp. The workers who had lived in this town many years assured the rest that the smoke was not a house on fire, or a rancher burning weeds, or kids lighting abandoned tires.

The camp, they told the rest, had not been used in years, the owner of it having died some time back. The mayor and the town council had gone out there personally, week after week, once the owner had passed away, and arrested workers who tried to live there free of charge. The owner, they claimed, had left no relatives his land, had left no one to oversee the cleanliness and operation of the skinny cabins in the trees. His bright yellow ranch house and twenty-six horses he left all alone and to no one. At the public auction, some workers pooled together their money to buy oak tables and a washing machine, and they carted home all the tools that had been rusting in his shed long before he died.

For several evenings, the workers at the park lounge in the grass, call out hello to those coming and going to town. At this hour, it is usually men going to buy beer. The married ones have gone home to eat, and the smoke from the camp rises almost at the dot of what would be a dinner hour. But these men crack open sunflower seeds and spit the husks in the grass. They are far from home and have no one to cook for them.

It is on a Sunday that they first see the teenage boy, followed by a thread of children, too many to count as they run at each other and into the street. The boy is tall, hair as dark as theirs, but his skin is too light for this time of year, and they guess that he is not a worker, or that he might be ill. For a boy of his height, his slender build makes him seem dangerously thin, and he walks as if bent at the waist, having been dealt a blow. He rings around the children, placing his hands on their backs to keep them from straying into the road, and, as this is Sunday and the workers are not working, there are more cars on the road than usual. Without saying hello to him, the workers watch the thin boy as he passes the park and observe that there are three children who obey him, walk patiently next to him, hold out their hands as if to reaffirm that they are the best behaved and need to be told as much.

Some of those children don't have shoes, says one of the workers, and it's this that makes them believe that the boy has come from the camp, with this line of children.

Because he is tall, the boy believes the children will obey him, and they do, though some of the smaller children give him trouble. At the camp, during the day, he does not allow any of them to run off for the afternoon until their chores are done, and he brings together all fifteen of the children, circled around him, his eyes on the ones who turn their heads to the orchard and its temptations.

Having no choice, he chooses the most responsible children and commands the rest of them to obey but, knowing this will not happen, he runs quickly from each cabin, surveying, helping with the sweep of the floor, the pickup of the garbage piled in the corners. One little girl is sidetracked by a naked doll, its hair clumped with twigs and mud, and he takes it from her and raises it above her head, tells the rest that they will play soon, taking turns washing the doll in a basin.

He finds this duty worrisome, his body always tired. At night, he must wait until all the children are asleep, which takes a while because some of the older boys want to sleep all by themselves in the empty cabins. But he tells them that this is not possible, that they must sleep in their allotted spots.

On the way to town, he wonders about how he will manage to keep the smaller children away from the candy shelves and the toys, what he might use to appease them. He wishes that his pockets were full of trinkets or pieces of gum, so that he might bribe them still.

There is a woman in town who owns a smooth-running car, the whole front seat a bench that runs undivided from door to door. She closes her windows to the heat of the day and turns the air-conditioning on low, so as not to waste fuel. Her husband does not attend the Methodist church with her, so it is her hat which occupies the seat. Later in the evening, as they always do on Sundays, her husband will take the wheel, and they will drive the outskirts of town. It is not so hot then, so they'll not need the air-conditioning.

At an intersection, though she has clearance, she chooses to wait for a group of children approaching in a haggard line. Her car idles as she watches the children cross in front of her automobile, several of them barefoot and tiptoeing with painful grimaces across the hot asphalt, some of them wise enough to use the cooler, painted yellow lines.

Before services begin, she asks several of her women friends if they have seen these children. One woman, wearing a scarf made of the sheer white cloth with the poppies, remarks that it is not surprising. Another says that the county should come have a look, but it is Sunday, so nothing can be done.

All through services, the woman thinks of those children, at times angry, at times sad. She thinks of her husband at home reading the morning edition, his loafers resting against the rug; her two sons, gone now, never without shoes, even in the summertime, when prickthorns sprouted in even the best of lawns.

Several women attend the afternoon tea arranged by the owner of the sewing-and-crafts store. Around the length of porch, talk turns to the barefoot children, and the car-owning woman nods now and then with self-assurance as questions are asked of her. She nibbles the cookies set out by the hostess, sips the sun-brewed tea, tells again what she has seen.

The boy finds that he is the one distracted when he leads the children through downtown. He tries to keep his mind on the pound of ground beef he'll need to bring home in brown paper and the milk and which of the bigger boys will carry the five-pound bag of potatoes. But the record shop tempts him to look. It caters to the workers via a small megaphone playing songs in tinny voices. Even so, he recognizes the places those singers come from, their faces smiling at him from the posters taped crookedly to the windows.

He makes the children file past the open door, remembering the bustle of Sunday cars, ordering the holding of hands, the smallest hand in his. At the sewing store, as they wait for a light, the boy ignores the traffic and stares at the white dress with orange poppies, flowers he recalls seeing outside of Bakersfield on the way north. It had been dusty, and after so many cotton fields, the sides of the road had suddenly bloomed in these same tiny flowers, and everyone in the truck had looked at them and pointed.

He sees the clean lines of the dress, how it must be handmade because of the stitching, the bolt of the same fabric tossed leisurely at the foot of the mannequin. The boy wonders who in town could wear such a beautiful dress, and where, and why, and who would take them.

When the small hand in his tugs hard, the boy finds himself surrounded by the children pressing their faces into the glass, leaving oily smudges. He tells them to stop it, to pull away, and then bends down to rub clean the smears with the hem of his shirt, leaving the window as spotless as when they first walked by.

There is another boy, also young, a worker, who lives with some of the other men in a two-bedroom house right next to the ice company. Sleeping on the floor of the front room, the noise from the ice company coolers keeps him awake at night, as workers are always opening and closing wide steel doors and shifting forklifts loaded with pallets of frozen fruit.

This boy has trusted the other men with his last ten dollars, remaining in the park by himself while the rest go to buy beer. He stays behind in the idle park hoping to see the boy with the children, because he wonders why he is entrusted with so many little hands and feet. He believes that the boy, like him, stays awake at night to the sound of the kids playing, that he must go, the way he does himself, tired through the day and restless because he has no rest.

When he spots them, he sees that the boy is carrying all four of the paper bags and the children follow along quickly behind him, as if he has only just scolded them and they are still scared enough to follow orders. From this distance, he can see the boy's face glisten with sweat, and he wants to shout to him or raise his hand.

It is when that boy and his children are directly across the street that he does not think and runs across, darting the Sunday cars. He hears the men, returning with the beer, yelling from down the street—what is he doing, where might he be going—and he feels caught, the boy looking at him strangely and quickening his pace, clutching the bags. The beer men keep shouting at him and he tries to ask the boy his name, where he's from, and why, but the children surge forward, carrying him off before he can make an answer. For a moment he is left alone, the boy and the children rapidly departing, the others catcalling their questions.

At night the boy cannot sleep, though he has tired the children with a game of hide-and-seek in the orchard. The children ran among the trees, climbing in them, losing themselves for a good long time before some started throwing the fruit which lay rotting in the soil, and he ordered the game over.

When he closes his eyes, he can only picture the young man at the park, dashing across the road as if he had something urgent to tell him. He remembers him as a frenetic force, his legs pumping across the road, shirtless, worked, deep dark from his face to his belly button. He had stood close enough to know that he was taller and the proximity, the brute presence of him alarmed the boy, made him open his eyes once more in the dark. And when he tried to sleep, it was again the round, dark face, the hair pushed back and not cut cleanly, the eyes oddly green. He blends him with the postered faces in the record shop, how the eyes begin to fade and yellow from so much sun, the music coming from a dark interior.

The boy in the park is again at the park, though it is Monday, and afternoon. The grass around him is spare and no one is off work yet, but he understands that he is not like those men around him. They all drink Budweiser or Coors from cans, wear white T-shirts that come in packages, are dark from work, do not smoke because they would rather drink. Some are from other places, some are brothers and cousins. Some work in the morning, others are like the workers for the ice company, keeping awake during the short summer nights with coffee and triple cigarette breaks.

He is a young worker and cannot stand up for an entire day's work, and the other men know it and send him home to eat before he collapses on them, the way he did during the early summer, tumbling from a ladder while picking plums, spilling the fruit, which the other men scurried to hide from the foreman. He is known to be weak.

On his way home, he had to walk the mile and a half from the farm to the park, past the lane which leads to the camp, the cabins a circle in the trees. Resisting the urge to follow the dirt lane, he thought of cornered rabbits and the way they kept still when he approached them hidden in the grass patches between plum trees, the feeling of the bones and fur in his hands when he picked them up, their hind legs kicking, the heart rapid-straight to his palm.

The boy is awake before the sun rises and it is quiet, the children around him so still for once. Down the lane, the taillights of trucks blink red as they move along the road, wink in the spaces between the trees. It is dark enough still to feel that it is night, that it is too early for anyone but workers to rise and begin the day.

But the boy is awake because he has not slept, and he closes his eyes to try, because the children will wake soon and not tire from running and not listening. He wonders if the end of the day will bring the end of his caring for them, if he'll be allowed to move on as he pleases, because he is older and can care for himself.

Of the children, he feels the most pity for the little girls, for they will be held close long after they will want to leave these lives. But the boys—as they do already with their claiming of the empty cabins, with the manner in which they scamper through the trees and feel no need to tell him where they are—they will go on without anyone.

The boy shifts to lie on his back and he puts his hands behind his head, so that he can see the sky through the holes of the cabin roof. It is lightening slowly, and within the hour, the children will surely be stirred by it. He closes against it and remembers the deserts of Arizona, the strange coolness of Washington, though it was summer and the strawberries hung rich on the ground. He knows that places are not what they are after a matter of months. Workers have told him of the monsoon rains that turn the Arizona sand to a silky mud, and he himself was already moving south when they finished the strawberries, and the wind, said a man at a gas station, was too cold for that time of year.

He jumps from sleep because he has thought of the boy who ran to him, found himself wondering where the boy came from and what kept him here. When he opens his eyes the sky is brighter, but the children have not moved, so the boy rises and steps out. At this time of day, the morning air is almost chilly, enough to wake anyone up without the need to splash water on the face, so he stands and lets his arms goosebump and folds them against his chest. Off on the road, the cars and trucks are making much more noise because day has arrived, and the boy does not stop himself from wondering, under the wide sky and awake, about the running boy and the whys and wheres and hows of him. He thinks of the places that boy has been, if there are ones he would like to visit again, did someone give him the permission to follow the direction he thought fit best.

He is watching the skyline above the camp, though there would not be smoke at this time of day. The slamming of car doors finally turns him to the county courthouse, where now inches a full line of cars into parking spaces, and several women stand near the palm trees, some holding purses, looking at the closed doors of the front office. So many of them are wearing some form of white that it takes him a moment to realize that their skirts or light scarves or headbands are not white, but dotted. They all seem to move in unison, pitching their ears toward the courthouse walls as if, collectively, they might be able to hear and know what is being discussed inside.

It is curious to him and he keeps watching, because there is still no smoke at the camp skyline. And finally, as if the women have known that he has been suspicious of them, they move suddenly into their automobiles, gunning their motors, turning their cars to follow a county sedan, a large green star painted on the side, leaving from the back lot of the courthouse.

Instantly, because he knows where the green-star car is headed and where the women intend to follow, the boy bolts down the street after them, running hard and feeling the fatigue almost as soon as he starts. His heels strike the hard pavement and then have trouble gripping as the asphalt fades out to the thinner surface, the gravel too loose in places. Up ahead the cars have turned, in succession, in the direction of the camp.

The boy runs through the orchards instead, across the uneven furrows, his feet dashing apart fallen fruit, small animals scurrying away from his presence. There are workers in the midst of trees and they shout to him that he is crazy, or that he should climb a ladder and pick plums just as fast, but he runs on, not knowing now where the cars might be or if the boy and the children are there, if he might intercept them.

He had not started lunch yet because he had set the children to cleaning the cabins and then refused to feed them when many of them fled into the orchards to play hide-and-seek again. They came complaining of hunger, and the smaller ones had succumbed to too much fruit and hunched with dropped pants behind the main quarters.

It is in the middle of cooking the ground beef and potatoes that the boy hears the rumble of cars. In the kickup of dust, one pulls ahead of the rest and stops. He hears the crackle of a radio relaying a message, and then a man in a beige uniform steps from the car and speaks back into the radio, looking at him and the children while he does so.

He is calm when the man approaches; he tries to gather the children who are not ill from fruit, wonders whether or not to put out the fire for lunch. The man in the beige uniform says something to him that he cannot understand, and the boy sees that he will not be able to explain, make the man understand that the mothers and fathers will be arriving any day now and wondering, that they all might miss each other as they head back south on the highway, the bordering fields holding the orange poppies.

He is trying to clutch as many of the children as he can, but his arms feel small. The beige-uniform man keeps speaking to him, though he knows it is futile. From the other cars, the boy sees, one by one, women emerging, wearing white, so brilliant in the heat of the afternoon against the green of the orchard and the dusty lane.

The beige-uniform man motions them all still and goes back to his car, where he speaks confidently into his radio. He opens his trunk and brings out a black bag and then walks over, opening it along the way and removing small wooden sticks. He counts the children in his quiet tongue and then draws the youngest one to him, who begins to cry, but the boy tells her to be still as the man pushes the wooden stick through her hair, searching.

The boy waits. The wide space around the cabins is crowded by the presence of this man. The women in white want to draw closer, he can tell, because some of them twist their heads forward, walk toward the cabins, and then hesitate. He brings each child back to him—how small they are—when the man is finished with them, and holds them tight and pleads with them to listen, though he knows they are too frightened to do otherwise.

From the edge of the orchard, he sees the boy from yesterday emerge, breathless and sweating, his shirt removed, and the women's calls of attention turn the man around to see him. With authority, the man barks at him to come closer, and the boy from yesterday hesitates, but approaches.

The boy holds the children's shoulders and the man, with difficulty, finally uses his fingers to ask if they are together, if they are one. He brings one finger to the other and pairs them, twists them together and locks them, looking at each boy to see the answer, does it again because neither responds.

It is the boy from yesterday who nods his head yes; he points at him and claims him to the man in the beige uniform who cannot understand. He hears the boy from yesterday speak and the words, though rough and chopped, inform the man enough to ask more questions. The boy from yesterday answers again, pulls out money from his pockets as if this is to take care of them, edging closer and closer to the group, so close.

The boy cannot grip the children any harder. He can see the eyes again and the hair that was cut too long ago, the sweat collecting in beads across the chest, the teeth flashing. The arms begin to tell the story as well, the man in the uniform seeming to understand, and the boy does not know what to do, because he does not know what the boy from yesterday wants, what he believes, is frightened to find out. He tries No to the man in the uniform, but the man has stopped looking at him. No, he tries again, and there is a moan from the back of their cabin, and the sick children cry out that they are sicker. The man in the uniform seems to grimace at the nuisance of it and then, reluctantly, turns to the women for help.

The boy watches them come, the white dresses and their sudden, orange poppies flowering with the closed distance. The man writes in a black leather booklet and he can hear the pen as it scribbles across the paper. Next to him, the boy from yesterday stands so near now that he can smell his copper scent, and when the green eyes look at him, he does not want to know any longer what it is like to be so close to things.

The Wooden Boat

My older brother, who's almost twenty and has a goatee that Apá does not like, has stopped wearing bandannas. He's sold his watch chain and doesn't iron his khakis the way he used to, the pleats as sharp as knives.

He's good to us now, good to Apá, better to Mamá, and he's been starting on me lately.

Sitting on a railroad tie tugged away from the tracks across the road, he takes a piece of wood already fashioned by the sun and the earth and the air and the water from Apá's hose, and it's enough for my brother's hands. He sits me next to him and lets me watch. The knife he says he always had to carry inside his right sock is for different things now, and he carves the fibers and splinters the wood, until a sudden, odd little boat emerges on his fingertips. "You like it, little bro?" he asks me and smiles, his lips pressing and blowing away the sawdust like the magician I believe he is.

But I couldn't nod at him or say anything or even reach out to touch it. Because as the boat appeared, in the harbor of his hands, I spied the dried flecks on the knife tip, and my mouth said nothing, but my heart thought of that bad guy slit last night, up the street, the sirens in the alley, the fading feet.

Loco

Loco Billy owns a house, or, rather, he used to own a house. And even the house that he used to own is no longer a house, just an empty lot for a year, and then tractors and men with hammers came and now there's a church that doesn't look like most would think a church to be. It looks like the county offices of downtown, dull yellow and flat and wide, the roof slanting only a little bit so the rain can slide off and not collapse the building, like the one in Orosi. The church is for Baptists and has glass doors that look dark against the daylight. The lawn is pretty and kept and the only reminders that Loco Billy used to own a house there are the great stone pillars that held carved mountain lions and the lost grape arbor flanking the building. The lions are gone, but then again mountain lions never roamed these parts. And the arbor beams are still there, but they do not twine circles of grapevine, only a strange climbing ivy that none of us has seen anywhere else in town.

All of us in the neighborhood could go on and on about what this church looks like, because it's there, and we can walk around it, or inspect it from a car window if we're on our way to the store. The church stands there every day, and its parking lot has cars that come and then drive away, and it's lit up on Sundays and Wednesdays and, since last summer, on Friday nights as well.

But Loco Billy's house is no longer. The days are past when we walked to the store to get candy and soda and Loco Billy would brandish his pocketknife with his good hand, yelling, cutting fruit that we think he stole from the stands on the outskirts of town. Or slicing yet another Clorox bottle in half, the handle part thrown away, so he could plant flowers in them and line them against the front wall of his house.

Those bottle planters, he filled them with his own yard, so that the lawn was blotched with his digging and brown. On those days, he had his back to us, and we could sneak by quietly on our way to get candy and soda, and there would be no yelling on those days.

Our town likes to think that it holds history dear, because we threw a big parade on the town streets with confetti of tiny American flags, and the council even thought it fit to invite the community group of our neighborhood. Some of our neighbors who are in the group thought this was very respectful of the town, but we could not find tiny confetti flags of green, white, and red. So we made do with cheers for the neighborhood men on horses and their sequined jackets, the hooves clicking against the street.

The town is a hundred years old now. There were old men and old women who were wheeled in front of the parade, on a float so they could wave to us from above as we watched from the curb. They were old enough to remember, if only someone would ask, what our town looked like years ago, that it wasn't a checkerboard of streets like it is now.

In the town windows, in the shops, merchants have placed giant, brown-tinted posters of the town back in the old days, and people pointed to these when the commotion about the old theater started. It is dreary and stained from so many storms. It is brick when we don't use brick anymore. City people formed themselves to defend it from the same men who built the church and were ready to come back with their hammers for something new.

They claim that a movie premiered here during the war, when Los Angeles was forced to be quiet at night and only the little towns far from the coast could see in the dark. They say that this theater has shown classics, has value to us, but lately it has shown only movies in Spanish of women with naked breasts and drug dealers, and no one goes to even those movies.

We wonder now, if only our town had held the centennial when Loco Billy's house was about to be knocked down, if people would have declared his house a monument, like his stone lions and his arbor. If people would have saved it, we wouldn't have to look at the tall brick building slowly chipping away and showing no more movies. In the old town photographs, all of us moved from window to window, hunting the brown pictures, saying, Look, isn't that Loco's house, isn't it?

Loco Billy himself was old like the buildings in town and falling apart. He kept his bad hand close to his torso as if it had just been hurt. His right hip jutted out, and he had to wear a special black boot to keep him steady, but he hobbled just the same, always looking as if he were stepping into and out of a hole. He wore a cheap cowboy hat and shirts that were not white, despite all of his bleach-bottle planters. He was the best person for stray animals, throwing them slices of fruit even though they wouldn't eat it, but they were not scared of him like we were.

He did other things besides eat stolen fruit and plant flowers. He stumbled into town with a wheeled basket and brought back canned food to his house. We followed him one day to the library, where he had to hold himself steady against the outside banister to the front door, and once inside, he sat at the circle table with books of maps and traced paths with his good hand.

It makes sense now that he left his house carrying a suitcase plastered with stickers of world buildings and the names of cities written in funny letters. But we know that he could not have visited those cities, only that he liked to trace them around and around in different books, because those suitcases were sold at the discount store, the stickers not really stickers, just a pattern on the grainy plastic.

He left in a station wagon, holding the door and leaning against it to ease himself into the passenger seat. We did not recognize the driver, nor did the driver come out to help when Loco Billy put the suitcase in the back. He had to push it in with his good hip, and then they drove away, and we have not seen him since that day.

We have all sorts of questions, like why a big moving van didn't come to take away all of his stuff, and why Loco Billy left his flowers to wither away. They might have mattered very little to him, since he let the grape arbor flourish but never picked the grapes, succulent and green on the vines and hanging. He guarded them from us until they dropped to the ground and the whole street would smell sticky sweet and spoiled.

The suitcase, someone suggested, must have held all the money they gave him to move away, but we don't know who they might be or where they made him move. Perhaps they asked him to move because no one really liked having him around, awkward in the grocery aisles and knocking down displays on accident. Or maybe it was his own leaving, dialing the phone and asking the Baptists to buy his house so he could have a suitcase of money for a place where no one looked at him and his grapes could drop and he could dig on his own, feeding fruit to cats and dogs that wouldn't eat his offerings but loved him no matter what.

We kept a close eye when they tore his building down. They started with the screened porch and exposed the concrete blocks holding up the front end corners of the house and not much else, so that the boards sagged. And when the front room was revealed, there was nothing there but an old sofa, dark brown, except for the places where the stuffing showed, and a couple of books on the floor. The men threw those things in the front yard, and soon we couldn't even see Loco Billy's flowers—the old sofa, the couple books, a kitchen table, two pots and spoons, a mattress without sheets, and that was all for such a big house. By the time the men had finished, it was all a pile of wood and nails, old newspapers which Loco Billy had stuffed away neatly in his attic, tied and stacked. All of these things they hauled away.

The people in our neighborhood like to know things, especially when sirens wail. Whatever might be in hand will be dropped if there is a fire engine or police car or even the lights of a tow truck fooling some to come out and look for commotion. We did not need sirens the night the Baptist church burned down because we could smell it in the air and from whatever window you could see orange and ash in the sky and people rushing to get a better look.

Honestly, our neighborhood did not care about the church, because it was a Tuesday night when it burned down and there was no one in it, because it was a Baptist church and only people from the other side of town came to it. And because of the parking lot, no one was scared that their house might catch on fire, too, from a spark that landed on the roof, the flames shot so high. We watched it burn, and the firemen with their orange lights spinning sprayed it until only the frame was left, and it was very black there for many days.

Weeks after, someone said that it was Loco Billy who threw a match on the place, because he was angry at having to leave. They demonstrated how maybe Loco did it with a trick of his one good hand, his fingernail against the flint. Or perhaps he struck it against his teeth, and then they imitated Loco Billy half running with his jut hip and his bad arm. Many people laughed at this and thought it was funny. I think we have grown meaner as we've grown older.

At the kitchen table, with the town newspaper in front of me, I told my mother about Loco Billy and she stood looking at me, perplexed, and now my brother—who countered that Loco Billy tried to stab him with the same pocketknife he cut bottles with—I move away from him, too. I've decided not to say anything anymore to anyone. They do not need to know.

These days, the place that used to be the Baptist church is again a Baptist church. It is still the same shape and size, flat and wide, but now they have put a large cross which lights during the dark hours so people know that it's a house of worship and should be respected. No one has tried to burn it down.

Every Thursday, when the town paper comes to the door, I do not read it at the kitchen table but at the back door, and I scan the obituaries, but no one named Loco Billy has been listed since I started looking. Of course, the newspaper would never name him as Loco Billy, or even Billy, such a name for a man of his age. I've searched for any Williams as well, but they have been lucky thus far. And everyone who has ended their days in this town has had a wife or husband, siblings of other towns, and grandchildren who can remember them.

Because of him, I learned a lot about seeds, about when you should plant azaleas and chrysanthemums, how to tell the difference between flowers that are bulbs when first put in the earth, how you need two hands to trim back the trailings of a grapevine. This one day, Loco Billy had not asked for help, and he growled when I tried to lift him from his fall on the steps, his good arm not enough. But it was there and then that he gave me two dollars in dimes, in a paper roll, to use the trowel against the yard and bring him dirt for his planters.

He showed me, in the palm of his good hand, the seeds for the radishes he was about to plant. I saw how, with his teeth, he managed, carefully gnawing away the top strip of the seed packet and digging his fingers into the container of soil. He could use his bad hand, too, but only to steady himself against the ground if he lost balance, and when I was close enough to see that those fingers could not grip, he sent me away with a point of his better finger and my money.

Please help me with these tomatoes, he would say, in a voice that was not gnarled like the rest of him, but a smooth lull, the way some people can speak to cats and dogs when they are afraid. I would pick the tomatoes for him, gently pulling them from the plants and wondering how he sliced them once he was inside the house or did he sell them in paper bags. I clipped the lilies for him when they were tall and he explained what March weather in our parts did to things so frail.

With great protest, the theater in downtown was demolished anyway, with a big black wrecking ball that thudded against the brick and dented the walls until they crumbled into dust. But it was necessary because we had heard of what happened in Coalinga when an earthquake rumbled underneath the town streets and how old brick could not withstand the shaking.

Some people wept over it, though I know many of them had not frequented the theater in years, but they brought home bricks that were intact, some of them distressed enough to sift through the wreckage, despite police protest, and lug away chunks of the marble facade. One man ran away with a velvety chair, purple but dusted heavily. If only all the town had done the same, perhaps the theater would remain in tiny pieces scattered throughout our homes.

I like to think we are good people, that all of us gathered at the theater during the wrecking would have done the same at Loco Billy's house, if the centennial celebration had only come early enough to make his home something to cherish. Maybe it would not have seemed odd then to want to take away something from his house, that no one would have looked at me strangely if I had kept something from his yard. But I would not have wanted his sofa or the books found on his floor. I would have hunted for seeds, dropped and lost in the rubble, ready to plant somewhere else.

They are tiny things, some flat and black, others pebblelike and pocked, and I marvel at how Loco Billy managed to hold these in his fingers. In the paper, they had a picture of the toppling theater, but I flipped to the obituaries first, but no news. I am convinced that anyone with scant lines will be him, small even on the expanse of newsprint, if he is still nearby, if he is not elsewhere. But I have no way of knowing, nothing to go by except his tending to small things living.

The dimes that he gave me for work, did he pack those himself? I have tried to flick a match with one hand when no one is around. When no one has cooked a meal and I must heat soup for dinner, I wonder if he could have opened a can with one hand. Did he press the can against the counter with his good hip to steady it? When I walk outside, I run into people who I used to be a part of, and they have babies in strollers. I bend down to have the hands clutch at my fingers and I clutch back, the fingers soft and baby-strong. I think of how hard it is to hold on to small things, the dexterity of thumb and forefinger, and these days I think of the care it takes to remove an eyelash on a cheek, or the delicate travel down to a hardened nipple—Loco Billy could never have done these kinds of things, all alone in his house.

It is too late to look for his lost maps that went nowhere or his dropped seeds or anything of those days when his house still stood, when we did not know how to ask questions that mattered. Like, who took those stone lions and why. Why was it that no one claimed Loco Billy, and who left him, alone, so late in his years. We did not know why it would have been important to catch all the small details before they escaped memory. The parade, the confetti, we could have caught some and saved it in little plastic bags for the days when we were ready to look closely at things, the tiny flags, if they held tiny stars.

By the Time You Get There,
by the Time You Get Back

There is a man on a telephone, a father placing a call from Los Angeles, listening to the empty ring on the other end. He has been calling since noon. The other end is in San Francisco, where his son lives with a man, a fact that knots the father terribly, but which he must accept because the son is his only child. The mother has been long dead and the father has no other family in the United States, and he needs money. He has been calling the San Francisco number all day, and the phone rings an empty space somewhere in that city. But he is patient. He has skipped work today to make this call. He waits fifteen minutes, then calls again, the afternoon hours going by, four calls an hour because he leaves no messages. It is a Friday afternoon, and he knows his son is probably at work, but still he keeps calling.

The father on the telephone is forty-two years old and the son in San Francisco only twenty-seven. Simple subtraction says there needs to be some explanation here, but there isn't much except the bare fact: the father had been young (obviously) and the mother just as young. The father and the mother had grown up in a small farm town directly in between San Francisco and Los Angeles, a place the father had arrived in as an adolescent, a Mexican national on his own who had been headed north to pick apples in Washington State but ran out of money in the small farm town. So he had stayed, and the farmer he worked for enrolled him in the local high school via favors at the administration offices. There had been forged documents with the farmer's rural address while the young father was housed in a one-room cabin at the end of the long grape vineyards. Still, under such circumstances, it became the town where he grew up, where he became one of the star soccer players for the high school team and gained twenty much-needed pounds from eating two full meals a day. It was the town where he never actually graduated, his English only enough to get by.

He lives in Los Angeles because what little life he built as a teen-ager disintegrated in the car wreck that killed the young mother, the girl who was never his wife. She was a daughter of the farmer who had forged papers to keep him around, such a hard worker he was. The girl had been sixteen and their little boy not much near a year old, but he had not been in the car. Instead, the baby boy had been sleeping, under the care of the girl's mother at the farmhouse, while the girl drove to her job at a doughnut shop in another town. She had dropped out of school to have the baby, while he (as a young father, but a father nonetheless) stayed in classes. It had been winter, the time when the farm towns sunk into fog thick enough to rival what books say about England (there is even a little town called London, population four hundred or so), and it was in this fog that the young mother disappeared, her car along a road so shrouded it was impossible to see the diesel truck suddenly in front of her, its red lights braking. In math class later that spring, he had struggled with the assignments that calculated the shortened distances and response times in chain accidents like the one that had taken the girl. How the math teacher, concerned for their fragile young lives, had warned them all about safe travel distances in these parts—the sudden closures of five hundred feet, two hundred feet, fifty feet, ten feet, then nothing but vehicles impossible to stop as they clambered over each other. He had kept his composure but struggled with the math and with the finality, too, the accident site long cleared of glass and metal, and how it registered for him only as pictures from the Mexican tabloids and their lurid (¡!) black-and-white wreckage.

The man on the telephone has nothing, not even money, but he values the papers that lay claim to his fatherhood of the son in San Francisco. It is what has kept him in the United States, able to work legally, and living in a tiny apartment acquired under his own credit. He knows there are so many people who would say that he has more than *nothing*—so many people he left behind in Mexico—but he feels that at forty-two, he is nearing an end line. Gone are the days of the cabin at the end of the long vineyards and the cold nights. Gone is the girl whom he should not have pretended to love. Gone is the farmer, too, who had helped him stay in the country, even for selfish reasons. He no longer has the afternoons during soccer seasons, the cheers of the small group huddled in bleachers because American football was the bigger draw. He does not have the younger days when his son was still growing and he learned via the bilingual woman at the advocacy group that he could see the boy on his own terms, and the boy rewarded him with hugs in exchange for the toys bought at the local strip mall. He has only the anger of the farmer, who raised his son, and the curious distance suddenly grown when his son told him (at age fifteen) that he liked boys. He has only the hurt miles between Los Angeles and San Francisco, his son who accepts his phone calls with a voice that is guarded and flat but never able to instruct him to stop calling. He has a job as a warehouse inventory clerk that he does not like and Friday nights at a cantina, where occasionally he can feel good about being able to attract a younger woman and bring her back to his tiny apartment. He keeps his apartment clean and meticulous with the hopes that this will happen. He has that at least, a woman every now and then.

The money he does not have (and needs) is for something he *does* have but will never keep—he has his own father in central Mexico, living in a poor village and now dying. He has received a frantic call from his older brother, still in the same village, urging him to come because the old man has suffered two strokes and is confined to bed. His brother's voice, dim and scratched over the bad connection, told him that his father had lost speech and was thinning into nothing. Their father would not be the same man from the last visit ten years ago. Ten years ago, he had traveled back home to the village to bring his father a high school graduation picture of the son living in San Francisco. He had shown the old man, healthy and sturdy as he was, the picture of his grandson, and the old man's face had trembled visibly before he allowed a few tears. It spoke to the old man, he knows, of a promise of family branching strong in some other place—grandchildren and nephews and pretty girls in lace dresses at Sunday church. It spoke to him of *having something*—here, the old man had only his cinder block house with one room and a stove; his wife (their mother) buried yards beyond the corn plot; his outhouse with the torn, tar paper roof, the letting in of rain and flies; the hook outside the front door to hang the caught rabbits, the skinned carcasses fanned all day by the neighbor woman until they were ready to be stewed; the bone-dry road to town dusty past his house, turning to a slither of mud upon the first rain; the stolen shopping cart trundled all the way from the new American store in the *centro,* mud caked on the wheels and the plastic belly but treasured just the same. The boy in the picture would have none of this and more.

The father needs the money to go back and rectify the mistake of not telling. He had told his father that his young wife could not get time off from work to travel down with him. He had told his brother that his son was living in San Francisco and planning a marriage to a pretty white girl after finishing university. He does not know if he will tell the whole truth, but he will at least go back and ask his father's forgiveness for having left and not returned with the immediate gifts of money and strong English and a wife who never had to work. He is forty-two and has not been able to produce any of this to his family as proof that his flight north was worth the risk and the loss of time together. He thinks maybe an apology for a lie can be corrected by the apology itself, though he wants to say nothing about his son in San Francisco and how his son's life means that there is end line in the United States. He needs the money to feel better by telling at least a half-truth.

He finally reaches his son at nearly six in the evening. "Hello?" his son asks, in a voice like his. When he answers back, "It's your papá," he hears the same voice but also the difference in the tone of its register. His son's voice is like his, younger but sharper in its command of language. It carries so much authority, the father forgets what he feels for his son—his perceived weakness, his dependence, a fragility. His son's voice harbors no such things. He finds it difficult to ask this voice for what he needs.

"Hi, Dad," his voice says to him.

He knows he should ask his son about his days, about how things are going, but he states his need. "They called from Mexico. My father is dying," he says and his son sighs into the receiver. He sighs his gratitude at being in San Francisco, the father thinks, away from such requests. He sighs the relief at being able to shield his life as he holds it in that city, that man he lives with perhaps in the room listening to this conversation. He sighs as if he knows his father is embarrassed and pained to ask him for this money.

"I need help," he tells his son. "I need to go there."

"We can fly you down," his son says, and in that short declaration, he reminds the father of the wide gulf between them. He knows the *we* is that other man in the room, looking at his son and knowing some version of his upbringing, who his son really considers family. He knows the man in the room is older than his son and is well off— he has heard it in the abrupt "Yes?" that has spoken back to him in his previous phone calls to San Francisco, his feeble efforts over the years to insist upon being a good, attentive father, though he rarely has anything to say to his son.

"I need to drive there," he tells his son. "I need to go by car," he says, because it is the way it has always been done, because it is the way he has always gone back and forth to Mexico. He does not want to take an airplane because he is afraid and because he does not want the difficulty of getting there on his own, the triple glances over his documents, the suspicion of a man like him able to buy a plane ticket—his son cannot understand. He hears his son sigh again, and he realizes that his son will never understand that traveling by car means controlling the destination, taking the best way there, saving the money from a gratuitous flight. The father grits his teeth as he waits for his son to answer—his son wants him to wait at a counter in an airport so he can say later that he helped him with the ticket, but the father needs the cash in his hand. His son still does not answer, and he pictures him in the San Francisco apartment, looking at the man he lives with, searching for help. *Cash,* the father wants to say, *money.* Anything he saves could go to his father, his brother.

"By the time you get there . . . ," his son says into the receiver.

"Please," the father interrupts him. "Please," he says again, because he wants to stop his son from thinking of the trip as dangerous. It is an arduous trip for sure, but not the way the son believes it is. Not like that man that he lives with imagines it to be, shaking his head no at his son. He knows that the man his son lives with thinks him backward, that he is a product of older, more stubborn times. And yes, the trips had been difficult and dangerous. The trips had been the long saving of money, the careful stashing of hundred-dollar bills well before the border—in the tuck behind the detachable but cheap radio; behind the flimsy plastic door linings; gathered hot and oily under the floor mats. The trips had been guards at the checkpoints with flashlights honing in on the U.S. plates, the car seat warm and sweaty from the heat of waiting in line, the dogs eager at the boots. It had been the cannonball speeds on the narrow Mexican roads, the suspicious cramming of too many people in one vehicle, the hope of not breaking down, guns always cocked and never holstered.

But now, the trip home could be about a return with sugar skeletons and powdery milk candy, nothing to declare at the border gates, being patient and hanging on to the U.S. documents, not letting them out of sight. There is an official residence in Los Angeles. There is a family member in San Francisco. There are traveler's checks more easily obtained than ever before. Things are the same, but different. "Please," he says to his son, one more time.

"Dad . . ." His son hesitates. He wishes his son could speak Spanish so that they could both make it plain. He could tell his son, in Spanish, to be a man and make his own decisions. He could explain fully about why he must see his dying father, that it means staying there as long as it takes, that it means possibly losing his job because he knows it will be his last trip there. Still, he has hope against the inevitable. His father will die quickly and he will return, to his own apartment in Los Angeles, shuttered with blinds against the afternoon sun. His son's apartment, the one that he shares with that man, is all windows probably. His son is staring out of one, he thinks, at the red swoop of the Golden Gate Bridge. *Who will you leave that to?* he wants to ask his son, that beautiful apartment, that life built with that man, but he stops himself because he believes it is all his son will ever have, and he cannot tell if it is more or less than nothing.

"We'll buy you a ticket," his son tells him with finality. "A plane ticket. That's all we can do."

"No . . . ," he tells his son, but his son stops him.

"Dad, please. That's all we can do," his son says. "We can get a flight for you for tomorrow morning. Can you go tomorrow morning? Will you be ready?"

In his apartment, there is nothing to sell, nothing to trade in. He looks at what is around him and there is nothing of any value. The phone he has in his hand is beige, has a heavy receiver, and is corded, its buttons gray. It is an old phone he bought at a yard sale, the former number still scrawled on the paper strip below the number pad. He had taken a screwdriver to it to prop open the base, to figure out why it had not been working, and resurrected the bell. His son, he knows, has an expensive phone, something silver and pristine close to his ear. They are two men speaking into a phone, he thinks, but so different. One is a father. One is a son. One has always struggled, the other will be taken care of. His son looks like him, but more like his dead mother.

He can hear his son shuffling paper. "We can get a flight from L.A. to Mexico City. Can someone pick you up? Can you take a bus out there? Dad?"

"It's a big city," he tells his son. It is immense, Mexico City. Even from the village, he knew it was there, miles away, gigantic. "Please," he tries one last time.

But the airport it will be. His son's voice commands with its English, the sound of the shuffling paper as if he scribbles. He says he will call to give him the exact time and to gather his papers in the meantime and to pack his bags. He says they will even fly him business class. He listens to his son's voice and agrees. He pictures his son on the tiny silver cell phone making reservations and fiddling with a credit card.

He hangs up and does not protest his son's decision because, after all, it is probably not even his son's money. It is that man's, the one his son lives with, and the father cannot do anything about it. He hangs up the phone with its heavy receiver, the feeling so familiar, even at forty-two, this sense of being held captive to someone else's whim. In the cabin, those years ago, he had a thin bed and a blanket and a door closed against the night air seeping through the grape vineyards. And yet, throughout that chill, he had believed he should somehow be grateful for what the farmer had given him. How to explain this to his son, this feeling? Does his son feel it? Did he feel it even as he shuffled the notepad and scribbled, talking into the silver phone, knowing all of it was made possible by the man he lived with?

It pains him that his son does not understand what it will be like to travel to his brother and dying father and bring nothing but sympathy. It pains him to admit, too, that money in his hands could deflect the hard questions about the pretty young wife of his son, the lack of recent pictures, what his son's house must be like (!). The father packs an old suitcase, taking more underwear than anything else because he knows the neighbor woman will insist on washing his clothes and it embarrasses him; he will try to do as much on his own. He keeps the old suitcase compact and easy to search and then places it near the door for the morning.

And though he needs even an extra five dollars, he wants a beer. He wets his hair in the sink and combs it back. It is early to meet a woman at a bar, but he wants a drink at least. He washes his face and dries it and then decides to change his shirt because it is seven o'clock and perhaps he can have a small dinner before his beer, playing patient with the evening hours, avoiding the phone call from his son that gives him the airline information and the departure time. He has no answering machine, no way for his son to leave a recorded message, and part of him sinks into the possibility that his son will become alarmed at his lack of answering, his worry as he listens into his slick silver phone. Perhaps it will goad him into sending a telegram of money later, at eleven o'clock at night when he finally reaches him.

But when he is ready to leave the apartment, his shirt fresh and tucked in, the phone rings with its heavy bell. He answers, knowing it is his son. It can be only him. "Hello?" he says.

"Dad, it's me," his son says. There is a whip against the reception, a hollow brush, as if his son is in a windy place and perhaps he is—walking outside of the apartment, away from that man. "Listen to me."

"Yes," he says.

"I have a flight for you. Will you write it down? You just have to go to the counter and ask for the ticket."

"Okay," he says, and flips over an envelope to write on the back side. He is careful with the pen and listens to his son name the airline, then the flight number. He repeats it carefully when his son asks him to do so.

"Dad," his son says. "I'm sending you some money," he says quietly, and now he knows his son is indeed outside of the apartment, outside of the reach of the man he lives with. He can hear the beeping of a car in the background, and part of him imagines his son on a balcony overlooking the city, the other man napping inside. His son says, "It's my money. I'm sending it to you, okay? It's not much."

"Okay," he says, and his son gives him the address of a wire office near his home and a number to give the attendant behind the thick glass. He knows the office—he has been there before, courtesy of his son. He knows the people who go there, men just like him, guarding the bills heavily in their pockets, looking over their shoulders as they wait in line. The young girls behind the thick glass, filling out forms for the men, asking for identification, securing numbers, pretty Mexican girls born in the States who speak both English and Spanish, taking money that is wired back home to the center of Mexico. He knows how the men then get on the pay phones to call their people, confirming the money is on its way. He knows the dirty tile floor, the men without money lingering outside, the occasional police officer strolling by. He knows the phone card advertisements offering rates to Guatemala, Panama, Bolivia, Colombia. He knows the duplicate offers in what is probably Chinese, the square-and-circle Korean lines, the Asian women hovering together with children firmly in hand. He knows the lottery tickets and racetrack stubs, the forgotten receipts, how it is mostly money being given *over*, not cashed in, and how safe it feels to be inside the door and waiting, not out there with a wad of money. He has sent money to his brother and his father when he could, but the feeling is much different when it is the other way around. The pretty girls behind the thick glass stare back at him when they count out the bills, wondering who is so generous to a man like him.

"Okay," he tells his son and cannot say thank-you because the words are inadequate, and he feels silly and incapable of saying them. He wants to hang up but must listen to his son hesitate, catching himself, trying to keep him on the line. He thinks his son will want to say something about how much grief he will take from the man he lives with, and the father does not want to hear it. He thinks if they could speak in Spanish to each other, then it would be different. He might be able to say that the dying father is really just *his* father and not his son's grandfather. He might be able to say his life has been so much bad luck—a girl he never loved, a son who cannot continue his name. He might be able to tell his son that he loves him only because of blood. He might be able to admit that all of this shames him greatly. Through all this, he might be bold enough to ask why his son still tries.

"Be careful," his son says, as if he knows. "I've got to go," and he hangs up.

With the envelope in his hand, the father vows to have just one drink, the smallest of dinners. He races to get to the wire office, out in the cool Los Angeles evening. He tells himself that he will come home early and rest and will even spend the money on a taxicab to get him to the airport in the morning. At the wire office, he waits patiently with the other men. He has not gone to work today, and he feels fresh and clean in his clothes, and the men ahead of him paw at their pockets, dusty and greasy from however they earned their pay. They have checks to cash, split between their own needs and the needs back home. He waits his turn, wondering how much his son has sent to him. The pretty girls behind the thick glass are there as always, directing the men to sign papers, urging care with the receipts. He edges closer and closer to finding out how much his son has sent, considers whether or not it matters. If it is only a little, does that mean his son does not care for him? Or does it mean his son is just as helpless as he is, under the thumb of the man he lives with? And what if it is a great sum of money? Is it a show of love for him, despite their distance? Or is it a way to wish a connection with the larger force of family, the blood ties that go back so much further than the generosity of the farmer who raised him?

When it is his turn, he hands over the claim number to one of the pretty girls and she asks for identification. She asks him who has sent the money, wants a full name to verify, and a relation. He says, *"Mi hijo,"* and she checks all of this and then opens a drawer. He does his best not to look at what she is taking from the till to count. So he looks at her, how pretty she is, how dark skinned and long lashed, how he might meet a woman like that at the cantina tonight, just a small meal and a beer with some of this money coming his way. The girl does not look at him looking at her—she is counting out the bills. He cannot know what she is thinking, if she is thinking of the numbers of men who come in here every day, filing away money orders and telegrams out of responsibility or love or both—which is guiding this amount to this man before her? And who feels enough of that urge to send it?

She counts it out to him, and he does his best not to listen. She counts it again. He keeps watching her face—how beautiful—but none of this matters to her. She asks him to sign in acceptance of love or responsibility, then lays it all out before him.

Anchorage

He is not entirely sure of the town. It might be close to where he grew up, where his father had not allowed him to return. Whatever the name of this town, he is living in it now. He has been living in it for four years. It was four years ago that the circus convoy stopped in this town north of Bakersfield, and the very young manager had sent out a group of men to unload crates from their trailers. They had unloaded the crates onto a truck that waited chugging at a tiny depot. He had not known what was in the crates, but he knew he would be asked to go along. He had watched the men unload old furniture from the convoy and then cram the pieces onto the truck. He knew he was too old to help them with such heavy things, and knowing this made him bring along his dark green duffel bags and his extra pair of shoes and his box of record albums.

The young manager had climbed into the cab of the truck, holding the door open for him so that he would sit in the middle, and another man had driven them out to a small, two-room house that had no paint. At the house, the young manager had opened the door and shown him the two rooms. One a bedroom with no bed, the other with a sagging counter and sink and oven. A tiny, dark bathroom with no window. "Are you leaving me here?" he had asked them, and the young manager had almost laughed. It was a poor neighborhood:

either large families or people too old to leave. "Oh no, God no," the manager had told him. "This is your house. Your own house. All yours. With the furniture and the stuff in the crates." The manager had looked at the driver. "Let's show him," and they had stepped outside to open one of the crates, and he saw them paw through sheets and cutlery and clocks.

He had stayed in the doorway, watching. His own two-room house with no paint, a sliver of unwatered lawn for a front yard. The young manager tore open a crate with rough young arms—he looked just like his father from years ago. Passing through this area with the circus convoy, the young manager's father had been looking for people to help with the work. He had gone along, his own father angry, to help set up the tents in Los Angeles. It had been money in his pocket. It had meant travel and his own tiny trailer to sleep in. Year after year after year, until he felt himself slower with the work, the arms around him younger. The father manager gone, too, by heart attack, and the younger manager appearing in his place to make things change.

And now, here he was again, in a town not his hometown, but close enough to remember it. In his own house that was not a house at all. They set him up with the furniture, a thin mattress for a bed, a waist-high refrigerator like the one he had had in his trailer, crates that would later turn out to hold only ceramic animals and many tablecloths. He believes the ceramics and the tablecloths had been meant for a woman, perhaps a horse trainer or a groomer—and that she now lived in her own house that was not a house at all, without these things to comfort her.

But the last item seemed to have been the young manager's final soothing token: a record player. He had brought it forth with both hands and said, "My father always told me that you loved jazz." Both men watched him as he received this last gift—an apology, he knew, a weak thanks for the years with strong arms—because it was clear that they had decided to abandon him in his old age.

These days the player rests in the corner. He plays records in the afternoon, the records he collected on the cross-country loops with the circus convoy. There were jittery performances from Chicago. He had banjo tirades from the coast of Louisiana, and black women singers. He went to small clubs whenever the circus convoy hit St. Louis or Memphis or Philadelphia, and he bought their records from people selling them on back tables, and he would tell them (all of them), "You should be playing New York City. Really, you should," though the convoy had never made it through there.

When he plays the records in the afternoon, he is lonely. The music makes him lonelier, and the visit from the next-door neighbor's wife even more so. She comes over to his lawn and calls out a hello—he leaves his front door open when he plays his records—and asks him to turn it down a bit. Their house is not like his—it is a nice house in a poor neighborhood, with fresh paint every spring, and he believes they live here only because they have no money to move away. He lowers the volume on the record player but does not know why she needs to have quiet: there is no one but the woman and her husband. They are younger than him: they are middle-aged. There are no children sleeping.

But she is not a mean-spirited woman. Many times, the wife will come over with bananas or fresh rolls in the morning, offerings he believes are small troubles made in order to check on him. When he considers their thoughtfulness, his tiny house does indeed feel empty.

He would know the woman Belinda in Miami, ten years after the war and his own leaving of home. He was drinking at a beachside bar where a group of Cuban musicians played horns and drums. She walked in, her eyes trained to the inside of her purse. She was searching for coins and asked for a glass of beer before she had even found money to pay for it. Her skin was patchy and pink and gave off a strange glow in the dark bar. When she put down the coins, she pulled at the collar of her gray dress, the fabric sticking to her skin in the heat. She did not sit down when she received her beer, passing the glass over her forehead as if it would cool her.

He slid coins to the bartender so that she could have another beer, and she turned to stare at him when the beer arrived; she seemed insulted at the possibility that she could drink so much. It shamed him, and he turned to watch the Cuban musicians, the horns tilted and calling to the ceiling.

But she walked over to him, to thank him for the beer, though she had only one glass, and he could not tell if it was the first or the second. She had blond hair, and even in the low light of the bar, he could tell that her face glowed from its sun-damaged ruddiness, the unevenness of her skin.

She said her name was Belinda, pronouncing it as if she spoke Spanish, the lilt not exact. She watched the musicians with him and then asked if he had ever been to Cuba, and he looked at the dark-skinned horn player and wondered if she was simply guessing Cuban but didn't know for sure.

She drank more of her beer, still watching the horn player, and she told him that the Cubans liked anything American. She said she was from Kentucky. He invited her to sit down next to him, but she refused. She asked him where he was from, because she didn't believe Miami was a place where people were born and then died. He said California, and this turned her away from the Cuban horn player, and she looked at him with her blue eyes and said the beach was nice at night and that they should go for a walk.

The man and wife next door tell him that they will be going away for at least a week, since the wife's father is ill and he is in Alaska. In his pajamas, he is holding the door open and does not know how to tell his neighbors that he is sorry. Though it is June and the South Valley is inching into the hundreds by noon, he cannot think of anything but pneumonia and how snow constricts the chest with its icy demeanor. He remembers a brutal snowstorm on the outskirts of Washington, D.C. He tells the wife he wishes the best for her father. She thanks him, and the husband leads her away back to their house.

He stands at the door, still open, and crooks his neck to look at their house. He expected them to get into their car and drive away, without suitcases or maps.

But soon the wife comes back, holding two paper bags, and she walks slowly across his lawn. Surprised that he is still at the door, she tells him, "Here," that the bags are groceries that she and her husband bought for him. "It will be only a week," she explained, "because the worst is over." It was a sudden illness and it spared her the agony of a hospital visit. Nonetheless, to sit by his bedside and help him about, she needed to go. "He lives in Anchorage," she tells him, "and it's actually quite warm there for June."

He accepts the groceries graciously and goes back inside to put them away. She's given him canned vegetables and dry-powder soups and fresh fruit. By the time he has finished storing these items and folding the bags, it occurs to him that they might have left in the meantime. He stands again at the front door but does not see their car go away, not in twenty minutes, not after an hour.

Clearly, he thinks, they have departed quietly, perhaps by town taxi, yet he does not want to close the door because he will face many days without a visit. In the corner, the jazz records offer solace, but he wants to save them until he cannot bear the loneliness any longer.

He peers over at their quiet house and wishes now that he had children. He is jealous of the sick man in Alaska, the wife coming to him as daughter at his bedside to nurse him, and he knows now that pretending to be ill is the best way to attract waning sympathy. He believes, if he had a son or daughter now, he would pretend to be feverish and incoherent so that they could indulge him with noise in his empty house. He is sure the man in Alaska has done that. He believes there is snow there in June, despite what the woman said. He pictures the man in Alaska on the telephone peering out the window at a height of snowbanks, and lying. He wonders if the husband and wife have been smart enough to bring warm clothes, and he peers over to their house, hoping they have not left yet.

Belinda led him to the edge of the ocean, where the waves came to cool their feet. It was warm because it was a Miami night, sticky weather, and the pink hue of the city pressed through the heat. He could see the pastels. He could see Belinda's blue eyes and her sun-damaged blond hair from the meager light of the lesser bars on the beach strip.

He did not tell her that he had a distrust of water, that the ocean at night, only a few feet farther, descended into an impenetrable black, the distant twinkle of ship lights appearing like stars. He thought the ocean held tremendous power. He granted tremendous power to the things that he could see.

When she asked him when he would be leaving Miami, he told her that it would be the next morning, that they would head up north to Jacksonville, all the way up the coast, and even then it would probably be a small town north of there, because the convoy was so long and they needed space.

The waves came in gently but made him dizzy. Belinda grabbed his hand, and they waded a bit farther into the sea. Even as it darkened more and more as they waded, he could make out the bottom of her gray dress as it soaked up the seawater. The current pushed against his knees. Belinda told him that she wished she could go with him, that there was nothing in Miami that was really keeping her there. She told him that she was not afraid of anything because she grew up in Kentucky, using an outhouse, snakes sometimes coiled in the corners.

He needed to hold on to something, and he touched her hair, brittled and scorched from too many hours in the sun. It felt even worse than it looked. He did not know this woman but knew that she was too prone to romanticism. He wanted to kiss her so that she would not ask to go with him, so that she would not open her mouth.

The sea came in wave after wave, Belinda's dress soaking and sticking to her legs, and she kissed him with a sense of desperation, he thought, and when she pulled away, she was about to open her mouth. He knew she was about to plead to come along, so he pushed her to kneel in front of him. With only her head to balance against, the dizziness of the ocean's tug and pull almost sickened him, and he thought himself cruel as he unzipped his pants. He looked down at Belinda, in the sad, pink, dim light of the beach, on the verge of being pushed over by such gentle waves, her gray dress floating around her, a darker dark than what was around them. She was kneeling and the dress seeped around her like ink, hard to see in the murky ocean. Her mouth was occupied with him and he stopped looking at her brittle blond hair and looked instead at the empty lights of Miami, a city on the edge of the world, and understood that some places allow things like this to happen because they are places where people pass through, live for a time, leave. Not like her Kentucky home, his California upbringing, where being born and dying in one place are such cruel fates. He did not like cruelty. But he knew what he was doing was cruel, what he was allowing Belinda to do to keep her from talking. He believed himself simple, but knew very well the difference between fate and action.

It is the third day since the couple next door has been gone, and that night he looks out of his window to see if perhaps a light will shine in their house, but none does. His loneliness begins to shade itself, and he recognizes it as fear, the look in his eyes in the mirror when his body seems to have registered its weakness and his own incapability to stave away sadness. The couple next door may not come back. Perhaps the father is truly ill and has suffered a relapse and needs his daughter, and he knows she is a good woman. She will stay with him.

He is angry when he considers the irony of being left in the Valley. He wishes he had shown signs of being tired and inconsistent in his work when the convoy was outside of Chicago or even Boise. Of all places, the Valley is where he never wanted to return, much less alone.

He recognizes, in his empty house, what his father must have felt years and years ago when he decided to leave the family. His father reminded him that they had land in Mexico, where they were rich from oranges and corn, that the land was going to be sold and he would inherit none of it if he left. His father put his boot down, insisted that he would be recruited for the war if he got near the big cities, but he left anyway, and he was deliberate in not waving goodbye to his father when he left. He left the Valley for Los Angeles, south and east to Phoenix, and started looping the country, and only rarely did he see the Valley again, because there were no cities big enough to stop in. But the young manager, the one who had rewarded him with the record player, seemed to harbor his own particular cruel streak and deposited him here, his family long gone.

When he looks at the neighbors' empty house, he considers the fact they are childless, but he envies them just the same. He does not know if his own family has returned to Mexico, if they have sold the plots for oranges and corn. It occurs to him that the man in Alaska may very well sell his home and move in with his daughter or, conversely, that the daughter will brave snow and cold to nurse her father through death. Though he is nowhere near dying, he becomes incensed that he will have no one to see him through it. He remembers the woman Belinda, but the distance of that time in his life is already something he cannot fathom. He reasons that she has returned to Kentucky and that, surely, she went on to live with a man who did not care for her. But nevertheless, she had children to battle against, she had a husband to contend with, anger to keep her company until her last days.

Before the convoy left Miami, he accompanied her to her small apartment, a stucco building across the street from a park where dark-skinned men sat out in the heat and stared at her. She told him that she was glad to leave with him because Miami had been bad men and she was tired of that life, just as she had tired of living for three months in

Havana. Living there, the Dutch tourists taught her how to say *guapa* and *cerveza,* albeit incorrectly. He remembered the Cuban horn player in the bar. He thought of the man's lips and his force and pressure as he watched Belinda unlock the door to her apartment, a filthy one-room with closed curtains. She gathered what she could into one yellow suitcase and called it her life. She bent over to click the snaps. She left a note on the door for her roommate, a girl she said was from Utah, a girl he would never meet. He remembered how crooked the writing was, but Belinda's signature was a flourish, as if she practiced it day after day. Picturing the girl from Utah reading the note, he imagined her standing still with the note in her hands, not sure what to do because she was as broke as Belinda and had nowhere to turn. He did not care. Belinda clutched her yellow suitcase. She was wearing a thin light blue dress with no sleeves, and she told him that she regretted leaving her job at the used-clothing store, where she got to rustle through the boxes before they were put out on the tables. She told him she always managed to salvage the terrific things.

On the fifth day, he has run out of food, and he opens the door to his house at noon as if he expects the neighbor's wife to stand there with more bags of groceries. He is perfectly capable of going to the store himself. It is too hot now, at noon, to bother; later in the evening, when the heat is gone, he will walk to the store and haul everything back in a shopping cart, which he will leave at the side of the road until the boys from the market come to retrieve it.

He feels abandoned and then simultaneously ashamed for thinking so. He offers the couple nothing in return for their efforts at conversation. The husband will sometimes water his lawn, sometimes cut it on Saturday afternoons, and then retreat to his own house without saying a word. They are a middle-aged couple without children; on Sunday mornings, instead of going to church like he would expect good people like them to do, they are dressed in white shorts and sun visors to play tennis at the local high school courts. They return before the sun becomes unbearable, flushed, and he is always out sitting on his steps, waiting for them to get back.

He is sitting on his steps now, at noon, down to an apple. Thinking he will eat it slowly, he takes a bite, but before he knows it, he has wolfed down the fruit, the core, and seeds. He flicks the stem into the grass, where it bounces once and then is lost in the browning lawn.

He doesn't bother going into the house to turn on the music. He is too tired. He does it to nab their attention; the other neighbors believe him to be a nuisance and are not as polite. Across the street, a family that is out of work is busy loafing, a brother sauntering out of the house with nothing to do, going back inside. A woman who he thinks is the mother stands in the doorway for a while, a loud conversation behind her, and she looks out at nothing in particular. She is a Mexican woman with dyed blond hair. She is wearing a pink nightgown at noon. In the doorway, she runs her fingers through her hair to smooth it down from sleeping and then goes back inside. He imagines her dyed blond hair to be brittle and dry and unmanageable, that only when that woman bathes and changes into clean clothes will the hair become soft again.

The convoy made one stop just north of Jacksonville, and he and Belinda managed a night together in his cramped bed. Before they went to sleep, she counted out a roll of quarters. She said she had no contact with her mother except packages of quarters, tiny boxes with rolls of the coins hidden inside, surrounded by newspapers. Her mother never sent bills, afraid they would be stolen. Belinda counted how many she had. She ran her fingers through her brittle blond hair as she calculated: four times ten times ten, the number of quarters she would need for a hundred dollars.

When he asked her about her need for a hundred dollars, she told him she was saving for a house. She would need nothing more than a little house, no matter where it was, only not Kentucky or Miami. Only a little house, with the barest of furniture so that it wouldn't look cluttered. And then she hesitated before she suggested California and the two of them.

They were outside of Jacksonville, and he told her to get a good night's sleep. He told her they would be stopping in South Carolina and, from there, it was best she go on. He turned out the light. He could hear her begin to cry, but he did not want to speak to her. He had always hated women like her, women who assumed living together was not a sacrifice for him. It reminded him of his father and his upholding of the importance of family. It reminded him of inheritance. Belinda sobbed, and he told her to shush, to be quiet. Between her cries, she told him that he was dishonest and without a heart.

It was dark in his cramped bed, and the smell of their dinner was in the air. She kept crying and he could not sleep. Reaching out to him, finally, she tried nestling her head against his back, but he would not turn around. She put her arm around him as if to say *please.* He relented: he turned around but did not apologize or try to calm her down. He ran his hands over her body and remembered the Cuban horn player, the Dutch tourists who bought her beer, any number of men in Miami who had leered at her, or had her, or both. In the dark, he rubbed her breasts, and she let out moans that still sounded like her earlier crying. He mounted her and held her head, her brittle blond hair. He was not tender with her, did not hold her after he was finished, but only got up to wash his face and hands. From his cramped bathroom, the light cast onto their bed, and she sat on the edge of it, rumbled and red eyed, her knees quivering. She went into the bathroom after he stepped out of her way, and he was asleep before she returned.

In the morning, they headed out of Jacksonville, the whole convoy, and he and Belinda never spoke a word. She fiddled with her yellow suitcase, with the fabric of her thin light blue dress, which she was wearing again. Around her head she had tied a blue bandanna. When evening came, he opened her yellow suitcase and, before she could protest, he took out her stash of quarters and replaced them with bills, and then directed her to the bus station at the center of town.

A week has passed. He hasn't eaten. He drank water and ignored the hunger, which was hard to do in the evenings when he tried to sleep, so he drank more water, and the need to urinate kept him awake at odd hours. In the afternoons, even in the tremendous heat (a heat wave began three days ago), he dozed off before the gnaw in his stomach began to trouble him again. He told himself he would go to the grocery store soon, but the effort grew more and more daunting.

But on the eighth day, he sees the neighbors' car coming down the road. He is sitting outside, in the late evening, the sun a half globe on the horizon and tinting everything orange. The car is coming down the road as if exhausted. He wonders if they have driven to Alaska and back but knows this is impossible. Travel, he remembers, took days, the expanse of places surprising sometimes. The whole state of Florida, he remembers, took several hours north to south, Belinda resting her head on his shoulder as they made their way north to Jacksonville.

When the car pulls into the driveway, the engine dies down with a shudder and the doors open at the same time, the neighbor and the neighbor's wife get out, the wife quick on her feet. Neither one of them notices him sitting on his step, and he is momentarily hurt that they would not consider looking over to his house to check on him. But then he sees the neighbor open the trunk and begin to remove large suitcases, and the wife, rather than going inside, has opened the door to the rear of the car and is talking to someone inside. The orange light of sunset makes it difficult to see inside the car: it is all shadows and silhouette. But he knows who it is. He knows the man from Alaska has been brought down here.

The neighbor unloads luggage and takes them inside the house, his balance steady for a man his age. At the car, the wife finally coaxes one leg from the interior and a plaid pant leg emerges. It dangles there for a moment, unsteady. The wife is reaching inside the car, both of her arms struggling to shift the man from Alaska. The other leg emerges and then, slowly, as if he had been bent and shoved into the car, the man who is her father stands and holds on to the roof. He looks thin and weak. When the wife begins to direct him to the house, he walks like a young horse, the legs buckling and unsure. He takes no more than a few steps before the neighbor comes back outside and rushes toward his wife and his father-in-law, and this way, all three of them slowly go inside, the car doors open in the dusk.

Later, just as he suspected, the woman comes over with a dish of macaroni and cheese from a box. It is night. When she apologizes for having brought over only a small portion, he shrugs. She tells him that her father has moved down from Alaska; they helped him pack his belongings in a few days and then flew back. The moving vans would arrive in several days. The neighbor's wife puts her head down to look at her shoes as if she doubts herself and says that it was difficult for her father to leave. He had his own life in Alaska, a marvelous set of friends, his own ways.

Without thinking, he tells her he has missed them, and she smiles at him and tells him to enjoy his dinner. He watches her walk back to the house where the windows are awash in lights, all the rooms in the house brightly lit, as if the neighbors were trying to burn away the dust and stuffy air that had built up over the past week.

He brings a fork from the kitchen and eats the macaroni and cheese, still warm. From his own windows, he watches them cross their rooms, arranging, preparing the wife's father for the first days of his final years. He thinks of his father, but not his brothers and sisters, and imagines that selling the croplands for oranges and corn has brought his father money for a caretaker, if he is still alive. He thinks of Belinda. But he does not think of her as an old woman, not his age or position. He does not imagine her with ungrateful children or a terrible husband. He pictures her on a bus headed from Savannah back to Kentucky. He is certain that she has returned because, despite all of his own efforts, he has been circled back to the Valley. He swallows the neighbors' dinner and is aware that he will die in as many years as the old man in the next house. That old man, too, has been brought back. Sooner or later, the draw of home lulls everyone back, he believes, and he scrapes the bottom of the bowl, still hungry, but fed. Across the small strip between their homes, he can see the old man from Alaska nestle into a comfortable chair, but he cannot tell if the old man is alone in the room. His face does not register anyone's presence. The old man seems sad and ready to give up. He closes his eyes to sleep.

If Belinda had only wanted a simple home, then this was it, he thinks, though he knows his remembrance of her has nothing to do with love. It has to do with children, with caretakers. He is envious of the old man. He is jealous that he will enjoy the comforts of his daughter's faithful giving. Though he does not pause to consider how the old man may have lost his wife, he dismisses the importance of having one. He watches him sleep in the comfortable chair. The neighbors flit about, readying the house. In Kentucky, he imagines, Belinda is being soothed and comforted. In Miami—for some reason he wants to imagine them, too—he pictures the Cuban horn player and the Dutch tourists relocated to Florida and the men of the park wheezing in their beds, the humid air making it difficult to breathe, and his only care for a woman like Belinda comes in believing that these other men had no part of her, either.

He goes to bed and sleeps. In the morning, he wakes at seven and goes to the grocery store to fill his refrigerator and cupboards. He makes a hearty breakfast for himself. By the time the neighbor's wife arrives on his lawn to call out his name, he has already been playing the jazz records, and he steps out onto the porch with a cup of coffee and isn't surprised to see the woman there with her father. Already, he is thinking ahead. Already: when the wife's father passes from this earth, he will fake ill, and call out Belinda's name in his most earnest voice, and when the neighbor's wife comes to tend to him, he will tell her how terrible he was to this woman in Kentucky—could she locate her somehow and fly her out to California—knowing full well it would never happen. The woman is there with her father, a wisp of a man who will wither away in the heat soon enough, and all three of them wave at each other in greeting.

Astilla

My friend Diego, because he was older, was tough. Not tough enough to live forever. When it was still rumor—that a shotgun blast hit his left side, that he had flown from the back of a car, that he was riding a bicycle and not looking—it did not matter. I was sad when I heard, only sure that Diego had taken the trip to the hospital, mumbling, gurgling blood, but not making it.

When we were young, we played baseball in a clearing completely surrounded by peach trees. All the kids in the neighborhood, everything we owned crude, the bases smashed chicken buckets, the ball ragged from a chewing dog. We owned the wooden bat not used anymore by the older kids, heavy tape around the tip to keep it together. In that clearing, where everyone ran circles, ate free peaches, it was Diego who did not mind picking me from the last of the bunch, and it was Diego who corrected my throw, got my stance right. He showed the rest of us and could shield the taunts.

The day I heard about the accident, I thought of that baseball field and the day the bat gave me a splinter. Diego took me aside, letting the game go on, seeing the long splinter dug deep into my palm. He saw me crying, and he pulled in over me like a wing to block all the joking. My hand tight in his, tighter when he pulled a pocketknife. With great care, my wrist in his hand not letting me pull away from the blade, he pierced my skin, slowly, and brought the splinter out, no blood. He made me kiss the splinter for luck, and then he blew it away into the grass of the clearing and our stomping feet. He made it better, Diego, who brought out both bad and good in us, made it surface without the expected pain, when he held our hands and made us dig deep.

WAITING TO BE DANGEROUS

Not Nevada

This man Ben is cutting the woman out of his sight. He pulls a small edger along the length of her figure and then slices. He is left with her boy, a picture of her boy, and he scraps what he's edited to the trash bin at the side of his desk.

This desk is lit with a large swivel lamp and slants down so that Ben never has to arch his back. He keeps it in the back office of his portrait studio; he never turns on more than the lamp to work with his photographs, the results of so much posturing. He's moved shoulders, tilted chins, wondered to himself why people have chosen particularly drab colors when he's advised bright or soft shades. In the safety of his back office—the bookcases and their crammed shelves, the cluttered boxes of negatives and unused film—he often finds himself looking at a fresh print and testing his own eye for symmetry. He'll look at a picture of a family of three boys, and he'll imagine dotted lines around what he wants—the second boy, his face made smoother by the finish. Ben saves what he cuts apart in a large manila envelope, and every once in a while, he'll take these out and all of the boys are there at once. All of their faces, all of their eyes, the crooks of their arms holding on to a now-absent figure, their sad and serious mouths.

A particular boy, with black hair, came in one day with his mother, his thin neck tight against an uncomfortable shirt. This particular boy's mother said to Ben, "I called you about a portrait," her tone already edgy, as if Ben had lied to her. She appeared to Ben as a woman that someone had indeed lied to, her face young but beginning to wear under the wrinkles forming across her forehead. "You quoted a price to me over the phone."

He told her the standard price for a portrait and wallets and said, "It's reasonable. Maybe a little bit more than Fresno, but I do them fast." Motioning up above the front counter, he pointed to the wall-mounted selections and their nectarine-wood frames. He expected her to say a cousin or a nephew was up there, as most people did. "Any of those formats," he told her. "Is this of you and your boy?"

"My son," she told him. Arching her neck, she looked up at the wall above the counter. "The price you told me on the phone," she said, still looking. "Which one?"

Ben pointed to the smallest portrait on the edge, not a locally made frame, but a manufactured plastic one, made to seem like wood. "That'll be this one, with some smaller sizes."

The boy appeared bored, shuffled from side to side. He looked down at his shoes, tilting his head so far forward that Ben could see the full part in his black hair. They all stood in their places, the mother looking up, the boy looking down, Ben looking at the boy.

"Okay," the woman finally said. "For that price." She stood in place as if waiting for Ben to take the picture as they were.

As they were—she wore a faded yellow blouse which, even though it was freshly pressed, drooped at the neckline, and the thinning fabric showed the vague outline of her bra. The slacks she wore had been black but now looked gray from washing and fit her too tightly. She had her hair pinned up, her neck exposed.

"We made an appointment, right?" Ben feigned, moving to his calendar, knowing from the woman's tone that he could not admit a mistake. "It'll take me just a few minutes to set up."

She said, "We don't have that much time," though the boy didn't look concerned, his eyes staring back at Ben in boredom. Ben could see the boy deliberately swallow.

"A minute," Ben told her, sliding over a hasty bill of sale for her to review and sign. She bent to read it, running her finger along the rates and counting on her tips, and in her deliberation, Ben studied the boy pulling at the collar of his shirt with thin fingers.

Ben knows that the people of the town are quick to think the worst of anything, and he has been careful to show everyone why he photographs not just the high school football games and the star quarterback and the defensive line but the town in everyday motion. Ben's portrait studio holds two front windows that display a variety of subjects: last week's winning catch, the receiver's pointed feet arched in the air; a black-and-white photo of a freak September hailstorm, with people caught in midrun at the lunch hour; the glamorous head shots of the senior-year girls, their hands around rigid roses; a close-up of a local peach orchard, the leaves turning into a violently bright gold.

This last picture of the violent leaves strikes the townspeople the most; Ben has always received requests for nature shots. He's trekked around the fields surrounding the town, capturing extreme close-ups of the plum orchards in bloom, the blossoms an impossible pink color, saturating the print. Ankle-deep in mud, he gets close to bees, or down on the ground to capture the fog that seeps between the empty vineyards during the damp days of spring in the Central Valley. He sells these photographs quickly, and people have told him that an eight-by-ten framed photograph is perfect to send back east—those relatives need to know that this town, this place, has seasons, too. There are changes here, they tell Ben, and he's snapped the essence of them, all the stages of growth, all the cycles.

The townspeople praise him, ask for more, tell him that he has a good eye for nature, the drama of a moment. For a long time, Ben had refused to sell one image in particular—the high school's star basket-ball player, captured in a defensive stance, his wide arms spread out and lengthy. The townspeople tell Ben they remember the moment just as he caught it: from a steal, the town high school broke the tie and won the game. As they've strolled by his studio, he's seen some townspeople eye the photo with envy.

But Ben kept the photo for its vulgar potential, how it allowed him to look at any part of the young man's bare limbs and see the already formed muscle. He remembered the game and the tension—and yet the moment suggested to him the star player's readiness to embrace his opponent, the other boy nothing but a broad, sweaty back. When Ben snapped the shutter, it was the other boy's fear of being so close to another man, his face away from the camera. So close, the curling of his spine from the possibility.

He had them sit on a powder-blue settee in a variety of poses. He sat them both side by side, asking the boy to smile, but he wouldn't. The woman put her arm around the boy's shoulders or held his hand. But the boy seemed more comfortable when the picture allowed him to stand while she sat, his hand delicate on her shoulder, almost with-drawing.

Already he saw the story in the woman's black hair, her fresh cut. He saw it in the boy's hastily purchased white shirt with collar—that this picture was for her, to remind her of what she had left. This yellow blouse accentuated her breasts, no matter that it was old clothing, no matter that the black slacks were faded. She allowed the smile to leave her when she tried to prompt the boy into holding at least her fingers, failing in these subtle attempts to convince him. Ben waited for her, hesitated to take those pictures, how she really appeared to the world.

"Let's take a few more," Ben said, and then rolled down a light gray screen so that the woman's yellow blouse would pop against the background. He spoke to her, to her loss and anger, to focus her at-tention. And then, in front of her, he touched the boy's chin and moved it to one side, holding it longer than he needed to. "Hold still now," Ben told him.

He photographed them, the woman not tiring, though the boy fidgeted and she looked up at him at the end of each shot, as if blaming him for the necessity of so many pictures. "Don't worry about him," said Ben. "It's hard to stand for so long."

It was like this for half an hour, Ben focusing the camera, at times taking long looks at the boy who needed the shirt collar loosened, his black hair. He imagined the slender torso of the boy, could see how his chest and shoulders were fleshy with potential. Part of him welled with sympathy for this woman and her loneliness. But he found himself wishing the woman to go away—he framed her out, had her remain sitting so that she could easily disappear, only half her body impeding his vision. The yellow of her blouse bloomed in the corner, filling in color when he wanted only the boy's brown skin, the hint of white teeth when he convinced him to smile. He slowly shifted the camera so that half of the woman's face was gone and he was left alone with the boy, through the lens, and he clicked these pictures, the boy's face alone.

"They'll be ready in five days," he told them.

Ben spends the next four days looking out the window of his photograph studio, as if half expecting the woman to come in and cancel the order or to ask something impossible, like a complete portfolio of all the negatives. But she never appears; she is not one of the townspeople forced to go on foot. Those people strolling by on the sidewalk, jobless probably, peer at him as he crooks his head over his window displays. They turn to look down the street, to see what he is expecting.

He cannot sleep. At home, he undresses in front of his hallway mirror to confirm his aging torso. He is not fat; he has no beer gut, not like some of the men he sees in the town's franchise restaurants. Ben thinks he holds up well, though the hair dotting his chest has begun to look the way it feels, wiry and tough. The skin around the shoulders has a dull sheen to it, as if his body was rebelling at his effort to maintain his Nevada build; he'd been a wrestler in high school. He'd worked picking potatoes in Idaho during the summers between college semesters. The Central Valley is oddly the same and different from his little town in Nevada, from where his brother had lured him with the promise of this small business. This town reminds him of being young, though the place seems absent of character. Even in Nevada, there were all mixes of people: blacks and whites, Vietnamese even. But here, there was only white and brown, only Mexico, only Oklahoma. Not Nevada. Not Cuba or China or Maine.

This anxiety creeps up on him periodically—this unhappiness, this uncertainty about how he's ended up in this small town. He curses his brother at times, wonders what keeps him here, why he is not eager to move on to the bigger cities. Los Angeles and San Francisco—both of those places satisfy. He likens them to Las Vegas, its arms open to comings and goings, the changing faces.

He considers cycles and permanence. Ben believes his acceptance of his place is not about any particular obsession; he never has the opportunity to talk to these boys as more than an intrusion. "For the sports page," he pleads with the exhausted wide receiver, and the town paper prints his blurry photos for twenty dollars. They come to his studio, these boys, when he has the courage to lie about fashion catalog layouts; he says, "Bring a change of clothes," and pretends to fiddle with his camera when they change shirts in front of him or drop their trousers.

But this particular boy from four days ago—he's nothing but black hair and brown skin, a face without much distinction—this boy nags at him because Ben imagines foolishly that he can steal this boy away, hide him until the rest of his young body catches up to the sharp spiral of his eyes. Ben has looked closely at those pictures, enlarging them, until the boy's face looms in a blurry nine-by-twelve print, his eyes perfect circles of depth and knowing. He thinks he sees what the camera is catching, yet not telling.

All through the night before the portraits of the woman and her son will be picked up, Ben is awake. He feels his eyes swelling, his back tightening as the need for sleep refuses to give way to the visions he has when he tries to rest. He thinks tomorrow will be a peculiar day, though it will be nothing more than seeing the boy's eyes come to life, stir in the way they cannot within pictures. Ben can think of nothing but vigor and movement; it does not tire him until well near dawn.

In the morning, though he had drifted only briefly into a light sleep, Ben rises and makes himself a simple breakfast of coffee and two scrambled eggs. He drinks and eats without being hungry and his stomach roils at the food. Later in the afternoon, he plans a trip to the bakery down the street from the studio, and he knows he'll have to eat again, even if he doesn't want to. Always he's recognized that hunger is the first impulse to leave him, and he eats out of a vow to keep nourishing himself at whatever cost. He remembers trying to make weight class on the high school wrestling team, sitting on the bench the day before weigh-in, his guard down, envious of his teammates. Nevada, though, was not always wrestling, was not always gripping a bench until the splinters flaked to the gym floor. To himself, he thinks something is lost by trying to forget the place—that it was a town near the Arizona border, that the town was a mix of people, the Vietnamese man who rode his bike at nights to clean the bank.

At the studio, he chooses a medium close-up of the woman and the boy and glosses the photograph, lifting out the wrinkles in the woman's face and giving her a vigor to match her yellow blouse. Her black slacks are no longer visible and she looks small in the overall construction of the picture. Her boy is lanky and vertical over her, so much taller than he appears. Ben sets the photograph with an unfinished nectarine-wood frame and then holds it at arm's length. He thinks, at the right distance, the eyes can travel only up and see nothing but the boy, the white shirt, his throat tight against it.

Deliberately, he sifts through the other photographs and chooses the worst ones for the selection process. He knows the woman will pick his shot, and he will lie and say that most on the roll did not come out right, though they did. Some have her with eyes closed. None of them has the boy smiling, and he arranges all of these between clear plastic coverings to snap inside a three-ring binder.

By noon, he becomes anxious and peers out the window. Across the street, he sees the secretaries at the welfare office trickle out to go to the bakery for lunch. They shake their heads at a man who seems to ask them for a handout from their own purses; but they point at their watches and make it clear that everyone needs to eat.

Ben closes his shop, sets the hands on the paper clock to announce his return time. The tightness in his stomach is beginning to match the knots gathering at the back of his neck. He thinks himself ridiculous in this small town, where his work is piling up a history no one cares about. That boy—he's bound to leave, as all the other countless ones have left, sometimes with a wife in tow, headed for another town. The space above his counter holds fewer and fewer familiar faces. Only the bigger families with enough children to create odds of some staying on in this town—those are the ones that point up and recognize themselves. Even from their distance at the counter, they see the shape of their own cheekbones and order their portraits, giving Ben a sense that they believe he saves only their images, remembers all of them.

At the bakery, it is the same people. The two women who own the bakery greet him, but cheerlessly, and he orders his sandwich without bothering to say much more than hello. He has photographed the older of the two; she has a happy life, with this business and her husband and their four young children.

His afternoon passes by too slowly, no one stepping into the shop, no phone calls, and he becomes worried that the woman and her boy will not arrive today after all. It occurs to him that she may work a midday shift while the boy is at school.

But near the late afternoon, as the sun has passed to the back side of the portrait studio and the street is darkened with shadow and his windows dim, he hears the front door open, the bells jingling. From his back desk, Ben rises and reaches for the portfolio even before he makes his way to the front room and the counter.

It is the boy, alone.

"I came to pick up the pictures," the boy says. "My mom said today."

For a moment, Ben is struck by the boy's presence, the arrogance never apparent when the woman had been in the studio. Perhaps because he is out of the constricting button-down shirt, the boy can slouch now. His shoulders hunch in a way that doesn't register as defeat, but boredom, a willingness to straighten up only for a fight. The same lack of smile now a threat more than anything else, his T-shirt loose, gangly.

"The pictures," Ben says to him, holding up the binder. "They're done."

"How much?" the boy asks, reaching into his front pocket. He digs out a folded piece of paper. "My mom gave me a blank check."

Ben shakes his head. "These pictures . . . I think your mother should have a look at them. We have quite a few good shots here. She needs to pick."

"She's working. She won't get off until eight o'clock," the boy says, and he unfolds the check confidently on the counter.

His misgivings about personal checks in a town like this; his worries that the woman will not like the picture her boy chooses; his fear that she will come storming back to claim he cheated her son with a ridiculous price—all of this Ben forgets as the boy stands in front of him, how close he might be able to get to him in the quiet of the portrait studio, the afternoon shadows making it difficult for a person on foot to see inside. He has a sudden vision of a desert winter in Nevada and rubbing an open palm against plate glass in a restaurant to see outside.

He tells the boy, "Let's sit down." He motions him to the back room and says, "I have a desk and a lamp, to see better," and to his surprise, the boy follows him into the dim room. He brings out the pictures from the binder and lays them out. "Look," he tells the boy. "Which one do you like?"

The boy studies them intently, as if he cannot figure out whether his appearance or his mother's is most important. He points to the one Ben had already framed but hadn't shown him. "This one," he says, and the finality of it, the readiness in his voice to get this chore done, spurs Ben to slow him down.

Ben says, "Wait," and brings over pictures he has stored away, the better ones with the woman standing next to her boy, not sitting. "Look at these," he tells the boy, "and these." He watches the boy look over the new entries, his face puzzled over the new selections, their better qualities. In the boy's confusion, Ben sees what he could not in the pictures. He catches the neck and nose in profile, the hair falling in strands forward, the large birthmark where his last haircut met the nape of his neck. "Look," Ben tells him, encouraging him to stay there and ponder so that he can stand watching him. His fingers feel like bleeding at the tips from the burn they suddenly feel.

And when the boy says, "I like this one," and points to the one with the woman standing, Ben rushes to find others. "Hang on. Please," he tells the boy, making room on the desk, piling picture on picture, and this time he brings out his blowups and his spliced photographs and he lays them out haphazardly. "Look at these," he tells the boy. "I can fix these shots for you."

There are shots of the boy's mouth, a long rectangular strip, the lips apart. There are eyes and half faces, the nose and mouth alone. Ben looks at all of them, afraid of his own misjudging, suddenly aware of his inability to lie and say this is the beginning of art and arrangement and collage. The boy stares at the spliced pictures and says nothing and won't turn to Ben. For a long while, he does nothing but stand at the desk, not moving, not even to touch the pictures and shift them around.

Finally, he says, "These are kind of messed up."

"They're part of a project," Ben stammers, and he points his finger to the front of the studio, at the window displays. "I do the orchards and the buildings. Art things," he begins, and he has the feeling now that this is worse than trying to touch the boy, even for a moment, the hot flash of his skin against his cold palms.

The boy is turning to leave, stuffing the blank check back in his pocket. "My mom can decide," he says. "I don't know anything. I don't know," he tells Ben again, and he hurries to the front of the portrait studio before Ben can begin another explanation, the bells of the door jingling and then quiet.

Ben stands at the desk, the scattered face shots in disarray. The boy's face looks naked, stares back at him angrily, in pieces. Every single one of his eyes on the desk stares back at Ben in multiples, and all of that accusatory energy temporarily stuns him.

But before panic sets in, he methodically takes scissors and cuts up a full photograph of the woman and lays those pieces on the desk. From the front office wall, he hastily brings down two portraits of people the town didn't remember anymore and he cuts up those, all the while feeling the front door will open with a threatening ring of bells. He lays the pieces of old portrait on the desk.

He takes his inventory of faces and legs and arms and, rather than destroying them, he scurries around the back office, tucking them into the thin pages of the phone book and the dictionary. He stands quiet, thinks he hears the sound of boots approaching his shop and pausing before coming inside to find him. These boys he never touched, only looked at. He captured them before they left this town and became old. He hides them in taped envelopes beneath the dusty underbellies of his bookcases. He scatters them as best he can.

Fotito

We're sharing pictures, the two of us barefoot in the morning sun, the windows not fixed yet to be opened all the way. I am flanked by a Cairo market, a ballerina midflight. I envy a flood of starlings in a London park, an opened castle. Here, an arched hall, its ceiling buckled up like a cat's back. A great soprano sings in there, I'm told.

I don't have such pictures, such places. Where I'm from is much like this apartment where we sit—hot, bare. My town holds only what people give it. Lines of houses, swollen and sad. Marble never made it to my town, I say, and we're too far away from the ocean to have thatched roofs.

We sit in the bare apartment and I'm allowed to fill it with quiet things. Tell me more about your town, I'm asked. So I tell about neighbors picking persimmons from their front yard, offering them in a paper bag. Apples come still dusty from the field. There are tiny frogs hiding in the irrigation ditches, dug under mud and waiting for summer to be over. They never sing, these frogs, I say.

The houses are rotting in my town. You can pull away the side beams, and if you're careful, you can put your eyes along the length of the outside walls and look. Look inside, and there's a family of wasps, wings flapping furiously, keeping the house cool. Until winter arrives and then their wings cease.

That's what it's like inside, a hive of wasps? Yes, I say, that's what it's like. We wiggle our toes, a triangle of sun on the floor. I look around—these are the sturdiest walls I've ever seen. It's hot and we force a window together. This room will be filled soon, with something like buzzings.

Waiting to Be Dangerous

You drove through the town. It was not like your town, but the people there were like the people in your town. They were Baptists, Sunday people, and proper. Your town was not by the sea, like this one, had no red clay brimming off the sidewalks. At the gas station where you stopped with him, they sold crates of peaches for fifty cents, but the peaches there were different. They were almost tropical, more red than orange. You were not alone; you were with him, and he told you to be quick at the bathroom and the old soda machine, the kind where you pull out the green-glass bottle of Coke for another fifty cents.

You wanted to act there the way you never acted in your own town. You told him to kiss you while he filled the gas tank and he refused. You told him that the people there ignored you as you went about your business, but he still said no and then asked why you wanted that kind of attention to begin with.

All along the way, on the interstate, you had made him pull close to the big rigs, their tall cabs making you feel low to the ground, and the truckers looked down at you, and you wondered if they did so to measure the gap between vehicles, checking for the white markers in the middle of the road. You remembered scaring your mother as a child, from the backseat, urging the truckers to blow their horns, sending your mother speeding forward, yelling at you to stop that. The truckers looked down at you. You were holding his hand, resting it on your thigh, and you wondered if they could see it. You moved it playfully to your crotch. You kissed his hand and watched for the reaction.

You told your boyfriend about the guy in high school who made money from the truckers passing through Kingsburg, out by the highway, next to the Denny's. You drove there one night when the guy's car broke down, and he said he'd give you twenty dollars if you picked him up. You drove there because the guy was your friend. And there, waiting for him to appear from the flood of sleeping brake lights, you wondered how he did it, why he never had the shit beat out of him in the dark spaces between the rigs, the oily puddles, the coastal sage along the road always rustling as the cars roared by. When your friend appeared, you could see his silhouette, and he was adjusting himself. He handed you, first thing, a twenty-dollar bill that was very crisp, folded over only once.

So where the highway was not coastal sage but palmetto, where the air was in the nineties and thick, where you were told to hurry and not stay long and not say much, what made you think you could be a kid again? You thought, *Love is what I can do no matter what town.* But you forgot that places just like these held things waiting to be dangerous. You thought of your friend's knees in the oily puddles and then of the bones of children cradled in the riverbeds on the outskirts of town every summer (it seemed). You thought of the green-glass Coke suddenly broken in half, just as swiftly as you knifed right up the road when you came to your senses.

After that, you kissed only when the sun set. You said, in the dark car, My friend did a lot more than truckers. You said, He takes seven pills with every meal. You swallowed hard, then admitted he was one lucky fuck.

Zapatos

It was sometime in the middle of the night, I think, that he must have tried on my shoes. My slippers to get a drink of water. And he found that we shared the same size foot and he woke me, pacing back and forth on the kitchen linoleum to get the feel.

At six in the morning, he pulls out boxes and boxes of his old shoes and tells me, Try these on. He has everything. Brown suede shoes that he keeps brushed. Sneakers and sandals. Shoes he bought in Paris. Shoes that are still shiny in their boxes. Riding boots from his summers in Vermont. Black shoes with squared toes and thick heels. Shoes he did not wear anymore, took up space, and he said, Keep them.

He is barefoot, in boxers, directing me, but not once does he ask to try on my shoes. He knows I have only two pair. A plain brown, a plain black. You don't like my shoes, I tell him.

They're okay, he says, edging a pair of hiking boots with surprisingly dirty laces. I say, These are not our shoes. I say, We don't walk the same. Because with him, as I catwalk for him by the morning windows, I can sense how the arches of his feet cave and give. He must walk with his hips jutting out to hold such posture. I think his toes must curl and then drag behind him.

Give me the boots, I say, and do not model, but imitate, thrust forward a parody of him, and he frowns, and I see that perhaps he paced in the dark kitchen because he finally found the sliver of me that has always escaped him. Because there, without me looking, without the light, he felt what it was to complain about walking barefoot to a corner market, to scamper across the hot pavement for milk, to buy only the fifty-cent flip-flops. He begins putting away his many, many shoes. He says he is tired, it's so early in the morning. He says that's enough walking for today.

Good as Yesterday

The detention facility is six miles from town, bordered by cornfields and peach orchards and on the northern end by an old airstrip where crop dusters rise up to cloud the fields with fine mists. Today is the first day that Vero has driven Nicky out here, her younger brother, a sixteen-year-old who cannot get around on his own, because in these parts a car means everything about being able to leave home. Vero drives their father's old Chevy Impala, and she is cautious with it even though her father does not care for it as much as he used to. At their town's grocery store, he has returned many times to find long key scratches etched deep in the paint; other times, dents in the chrome from someone's jealous, hard-kicking boots. He does not wash and wax the car as before, does not scour local dealers for repairs and parts, does not spend the time honing the engine. Not to see his car treated that way. So he lets Vero use it to drive around town and here she is, easing slowly into the parking lot of the detention facility because the lot is only a large square of gravel and railroad ties to bump tires against. The low fields are all around them, and a duster lazily drones off from the airstrip as Vero stops the car. She wonders if the air ever blows the pesticides into the parking lot, into the dirt courtyard of the detention facility where these Sunday visits are held.

Her younger brother Nicky is ready to get out of the car before she quits the ignition. He has his fingers on the door handle and holds a Macy's shopping bag between his legs. He has made Vero drive him to the mall in Fresno so that he could ask for a paper shopping bag, the kind with the small loops at the top, even though he did not buy anything. Macy's is the nicest store around, and for this visit, her little brother wants to enter the detention facility with a measure of attention, even though the Macy's bag holds nothing but a bucket of fried chicken and store-bought rolls and little packets of butter, the knives and forks that come in separate plastic packages. He has bought a six-pack of Cokes and a stack of paper plates, though they will only use three.

Sunday afternoons are lunch visitations in the courtyard, sitting on picnic benches that look like they belong in a playground or a school, not a detention facility. There are full, shady trees in the courtyard, but no green grass, and the facility officers hose down the dust before the family arrivals. Already, there is a line of people with ice chests and grocery bags waiting patiently in the heat. Near the entrance, a blue tarp is strung taut over the door for shade, and beyond that, Vero can see the green-gray uniforms of the detainees as they peer from the windows, patient in the long barracks across the courtyard.

To say there is a line of people is inexact: there is a line of women, mostly young ones, Vero's age. Vero is twenty years old, four years older than her little brother, but she feels the saddled burdens that must (she thinks) be the lives of the young women just like her standing in line. They are young women with babies in tow, mothers once if not twice, but she does not recognize any of them from her own town. The detention facility is for the northern part of the county, a holding place for people of the most minor offenses—vandalism and bar brawls, excessive speeding violations, drunken driving, child-support evasion—all bad things to Vero, but common in her town and in the towns where these women are from. Ivanhoe and Tulare, Yettem and Cutler, Exeter and Lindsay. She is grateful that she is twenty but not completely like them.

She is in no rush to get inside the facility, but Nicky hurries. He is walking quickly with the Macy's shopping bag in his left hand, the other hand extended out. She hates to see his hand extended out like that, his exaggerations, his boldness at sixteen. Inside the bag, Nicky has brought more than food. He has brought cookies and magazines, though Vero has warned him that the detention facility would probably prohibit gifts. Nicky has walked every day after school to buy greeting cards from the drugstore in the center of their downtown, and he has spent long hours writing his messages and sealing them away. He has gone into the small crafts store that sells nectarine-wood frames and expensive glassware and has purchased bright orange ribbon, taking scissors to it and curling the edges, bundling up the greeting cards. The cards with the ribbon are in the bag.

Nicky is standing in line already, still a few minutes from the inspection point but impatient. She hears his voice echo, "Come on!" and the other people in line turn around to look at him. He has cards to give; the chicken is already cold. He is sixteen years old and cannot wait any longer.

Vero walks forward. The voices of her friends keep chiding her. *You do too much for that brother of yours, Vero. Let him be his own.* She stands and waits with him. Her feet hurt. She has a job at the auto parts store in downtown, a family-owned business losing out to the new strip mall, a job where she stands all day at a counter. She is twenty and unmarried in a place where most have either left or married by that age, and she knows so many of the men in town from the store. They look for parts to repair a wife's car, a cousin's work truck, stepping into the shop with its cement floor and the loud rotary fans hung high in the ceiling, the cool chemical smells of lubricant and oil and new rubber. They buy spark plugs and fan belts, handing them over to her with hands just as smooth and young as hers, the wedding bands glimmering. She could have it worse, she knows. She could lose the job if the strip mall takes away too much business. She would have to move to another town for work, she knows, and then what? How long can the

Impala run without her father fixing it as he used to? What would happen to her little brother if she were not around?

They inch closer and closer to the guard, and when they arrive, the guard turns to Vero as if he recognizes that she is the older sibling and asks, "Who are you here to see?"

"Julián Orosco," she says. Nicky is holding the bag to himself, as if he does not want the guard to see, but the guard waves him to open it and peeks inside, reaching in to move things around. The guard is an old man and takes his time. He opens the bucket of chicken and closes it. He shifts between the store-bought rolls and the butter and the plastic. When he sees the bundle of cards, he says, "Those out, please," and Nicky takes them out. "Unwrap them, please," he orders and Nicky looks down at the orange ribbon, snug so tight around the envelopes that it has made little bends in the paper, and then he does his best to push one of the loops off the edge to keep the ribbon intact.

The guard takes the bundle from Nicky, and Vero sees his old hands run through each one, thumb and forefinger, feeling for anything suspiciously thick. She can read Nicky's pretty writing: JULIÁN and MI AMOR and SIEMPRE NICOLÁS and the intricate hearts he has sketched on the back flaps, brooding and pulsing fleshy hearts with blood dripping like sweat.

"You can't bring in anything sealed," the guard says finally. "You'll have to open these." Behind them, Vero can hear the shifting of someone impatient with both the old man's adherence to rules and Nicky's foolishness in bringing the cards in the first place. Nicky looks pained and when he turns to Vero to begin his protest, she gives him a look that says, *Do it.* It is not the way he wanted it to be: these cards are for Julián Orosco, the man he thinks he loves, and he hesitates.

So Vero takes the cards and begins unsealing them, handing them over to the old guard, who looks inside each one attentively. She is careful not to rip the envelopes completely, and it pains her that she is doing this for her little brother. There are fifteen cards in all, and she does the math in her head, the money he has spent for this visit: the cards and the chicken, the cookies and the magazines. She has given him spending money. She has made too much of this possible.

Satisfied, the old guard hands the cards back, and Vero cannot look at Nicky as he struggles to put the ribbon back in place. Behind them is the rustle of irritation. Nicky cannot get the ribbon to fit again, but she waits patiently for him to finish because she knows that when he sees Julián, he wants everything to be in order.

Their mother never liked Julián. She never liked him because he wore the cheap, tight muscle shirts that came out of the package, the cotton fabric thin enough to see his dark nipples underneath. He wore his pants low to show his boxers, and their mother frowned at what it all suggested. Vero had brought him to the house, not to introduce him but to show her parents that she was twenty and could do what she wanted—she was a grown woman and here was a guy her age who had his own job and apartment. She had not told their mother that she had met Julián at a party and that he had invited her to the backyard where there was no light and she had let him come on the inside of her leg while they were pushed up against the fence. Their mother is not a churchgoer or a bitter divorced woman like so many in their neighborhood. Their mother is pretty—a heavy woman and tall and imposing, but pretty—a conservative force in the house. She had looked at Julián without offering to bring him a drink and left the living room. Their father had already left the room: he stayed out of the way of visitors. Their father had not been like Julián; their father had been the churchgoer, though their mother had made him stop going.

If Vero had had any hesitations about bringing Julián to the house, it had to do with Nicky. Nicky had changed lately. He had been giving their parents a lot of lip, though their father never was one to push things. It was their mother who demanded better manners and punished him with curfews, but Nicky defied her every chance he had. He stayed out late with his new group of friends. He spent the money he had from his own part-time job as a stockboy on clothes and movies and then demanded money for lunch, and it was their father who gave it to him because their father never liked yelling in the house.

Nothing could have happened between Julián and Nicky on that first day, but Vero always imagined that something had. She had never left the room. Nothing had happened except hello. But she knew Nicky had stared too long at Julián, that he had shaken Julián's hand in the many-fisted way that Julián shook hands. And he had shaken hands that way because Vero knew that Nicky had wanted to touch him. He had wanted to touch his broad shoulders and the tight chest peeking through his white muscle shirt. It would be later in life that she would admit that their mother had wanted to do the same thing, that the gold chain and the brown skin and the hairless chest had reminded their mother of her girl days when she did not pay her own parents mind. Nicky had wanted to do these things; their mother had; Vero had. Later, angry at Nicky, she had wanted to believe that Julián stood in their living room and looked Nicky up and down, thirsting for the easiness of a sixteen-year-old, not caring that she was in the room.

To not anger their mother, Vero lies about their visit to the detention center and tells her that they will be going to the mall to buy Nicky clothes, but their mother is angry anyway. "Why does that boy need more clothes?" she asks, not looking at Vero, not looking at Nicky, who is in the room. She is flipping through the television stations because Sunday on Spanish television is bad movies or *fútbol* soccer and she doesn't like either. "*¿Con que dinero?*" she asks the television, and Nicky says he has money and goes back to his room so that he can tuck the cards with orange ribbon under his shirt.

Vero's friends resent what Nicky gets away with. They warn her that Nicky is looking to get another beating, the way he walks around in school, haughty in his new clothes. Vero ignores her friends when they complain because she cannot tell them simply that she loves her younger brother. Because she sometimes thinks that she doesn't. She doesn't love him when he tells her that she is like their mother—heavy and tall and imposing, but pretty. She doesn't love him when he complains about their parents and how much they don't love him. She wants to tell him that they do, but the simplicity of love is too difficult: she wants to tell him, sometimes he is loved and sometimes he is not. He is loved and then not loved because he can be petulant and arrogant.

She has always wanted to tell him that she loves him because of how he came home on his sixteenth birthday. He had come home running. He had come home bleeding. In one of the alleys in their neighborhood, six boys had dragged and beaten him. All six of them had taken turns, boys he went to school with, boys from another neighborhood, boys he grew up with, boys he had secretly fooled with on back porches. Gaudio, Peter, Alex, Fidel, Israel, and Andy. They had said they were tired of him. And when their mother had tried to calm him down, saying, "Who did this to you? Why did they do this to you? Why?" Vero had known that their mother did not know anything about Nicky and how the cuts and deep bruises spelled out who he really was. Her friends had warned her: *Tell your little brother to stop acting like that. Tell him to stop looking at the guys like that. They don't think it's funny.* Nicky had been sobbing, and he had spat out a thin mixture of blood and saliva into the bathroom sink, and Vero had tried to clean him up. She had wanted to tell him that it was okay and that she loved him, but he had his head bent down and cried the way the mothers and grandmothers did at funerals. He had his head down, and she had felt like their mother, looking at his beautiful black hair, the cuts on his ears, the scratches on his neck. She wondered why on earth he believed he could act like this with the boys at the high school and not expect this outcome. She could see dark spots on the cloth of his shirt, and she made him take it off—more cuts, more blood, bruises as purple-deep as orchard plums, yellowing in some places. "Nicky," she had said, but that was all she said. She motioned for him to get in the shower, and he rose slowly to close the door so that he could take off the rest of his clothes and clean himself.

Vero does not want to sit at the picnic tables and eat. She watches Julián and he watches her back, though he is no longer ashamed like he used to be. There are other families around, the girls her age from other towns with kids running circles around their tables, kicking up the watered-down dust in the courtyard. Everywhere there is food and two-liter soda bottles, foil and aluminum cans, and men in gray-green shirts like Julián. None of them looks dangerous. Vero turns away from Julián and Nicky, who is taking out the food from the Macy's bag, and she studies the men in gray-green shirts. Like Julián, they are here for something stupid and small. They are here making the girls her age sadder than they already are for having their kids. There is one who is skinny, with a goatee and his hair slicked back, looking uncomfortable and sunken in the gray-green shirt, and the family around him seems to kid and pity him at the same time.

"Vero, come eat," she hears Nicky say to her, and she turns back to Julián and her younger brother. She can see the greeting cards on the table.

Nicky serves them, gives Julián three pieces of chicken, piles his paper plate with the store-bought rolls. He is enjoying this display, feeding his man, imitating the aunts in their family who linger in the kitchen and bring out hot plates to the uncles. She knows the people around them subscribe to this way of thinking, too, and she wonders if they are looking over at Nicky and wondering why he is doing the work and not her. Julián eats before them and Vero finally speaks to him directly, because she still finds him difficult and Julián was never much of a talker in the first place. "They're not feeding you anything good, huh?"

"Umum," Julián says, and keeps eating.

"What do they make you do?" Nicky asks.

"Nothing. I don't do anything all day. Just sit around. Play poker."

He will be here for two months because of unpaid traffic tickets. That was all. They had caught him speeding late one night south of Fresno, and Vero remembers the phone call to their house, their mother peeking from the bedroom door to make sure it wasn't a dead relative in Mexico, and Julián saying, "I gotta talk to Nicky. Put him on, Vero." And Nicky cried over the few tickets like it was the end of the world. "You're where? For how long?"

"It's just the food that's a bitch," Julián says, taking another piece of chicken, another roll.

Around them, the families are tossing trash and clearing the picnic tables. They are sipping soda. The children at every table look bored, the courtyard nothing but dirt and shade. The families are talking quietly. Not many of them are laughing.

Nicky begins. He pushes the bundle of letters over to Julián and says, "These are for you, Julián. The guard made me open them." Vero wants to leave, but around them is nothing but the other families, all the tables occupied. In the parking lot, there would be nothing but the old airfield.

"I want you to open one up in the morning and then another one at night before you go to sleep," Nicky says. "Promise."

Vero turns away. She hears Julián say, "Nicky . . ." in that hesitant voice, the kind that anyone in love cannot recognize as frustration. She hopes Nicky will be quiet for his own sake.

"I love you, Julián," Nicky says, and she can tell Julián is trying his best to pull away from the table as Nicky leans forward. Vero herself looks around to see if people are listening but doesn't wait. She is embarrassed by this as much as Julián. "That's enough, Nicky," she says softly, and Nicky says no more.

When they leave, Nicky is in tears because Julián did not hug him, only patted him on the shoulders like a brother and then tucked the bundle of cards under his armpit and made his way back to the barracks.

"Nicky," she begins, "you better calm down before we get home." She wants to tell him to shape up, that Julián only has a matter of a few weeks, but it is his first real love and so she lets him. She tells herself that she is doing the right thing, that she can ignore her own humiliation at having her younger brother carry on like this with someone she has known intimately. She tells herself that she is stronger, that ultimately she has more options than someone like Nicky will ever have in a place like this, and that she is twenty and she could be like the girls from Cutler and Ivanhoe.

Because he is still crying, Vero drives the car toward Fresno. They will go to the mall and walk around in the air-conditioning until he calms down. When they reach Highway 99 and can go faster, Nicky leans back as if he knows where they are going.

"No stealing," she tells him because Nicky has done it before, every now and then. A shirt he's stuffed into his pants. A CD or two after he put electrical tape over the bar code. Even the greeting cards, she knows, were not all honest purchases. Vero has not shared this with their parents. It is one of the ways that Nicky changed after he was jumped by the boys he grew up with. He's become more brazen with everything but has yet to face consequences. He had to walk around school with deep, red rings around his eyes as the bruises healed there, his lips swollen. Then one morning, he went to school without trying to blend Vero's makeup around his wounds. He left it thick and noticeable and walked out of the house sullenly. He came back home at the end of the day just fine.

"I won't steal a thing," Nicky promises.

Her friends (always her friends) told her what Nicky had done. They had seen Julián's car at the old drive-in. His car had pulled in about ten-thirty, and he had to park in front because the back of the lot was full. They told Vero they were sure it was Julián's car. They saw

Nicky go to the concession stand and come back out with big Styrofoam cups of Coke and a bucket of popcorn. They saw Julián leave the car later to go the bathroom: *Vero,* they told her, *both of them were there together.*

"What movie?" she had asked them because it had been a long time since she had gone to the drive-in, even though it still did business.

Why does that matter? they told her back. *Who cares?* They wanted to know what she was going to tell Julián.

"You can't prove anything," she had told them, and all of them huffed because they had been at the drive-in, open only on Sunday nights after the flea market, and they knew why people went there.

At the mall, Vero leads Nicky to a bookstore because Nicky takes too long to look at clothes and she wants to avoid that. Vero sifts through the magazines and they stand there flipping through all the pages. Nicky picks up the teen-girl magazines with the pictures of blond boys on the cover. "Put that down, Nicky," she tells him, and he does, wandering off.

When she finds him later, he is in front of a display of movie books, the big thick expensive books with glossy black-and-white pictures. "Do you know who this is?" Nicky asks and holds up a picture of Bette Davis.

"Bette Davis," Vero tells him, because her name is scrolled underneath.

"How about her?" he asks, flipping pages and stopping on a studio shot of *A Streetcar Named Desire.*

"Vivien Leigh," says Vero, because she recognizes her from watching the afternoon movies on channel 26, and then she points at the woman standing next to Blanche DuBois.

"Do you know who Kim Hunter is?" Vero asks.

"Not really," Nicky says. He has done this before: he rented an old Joan Crawford movie once because he thought he was supposed to like her. But he turned it off after twenty minutes and said, "This is so fucking boring."

At home their mother does not ask them where they have been but complains that they have been gone all day. Their father sits in the living room watching *fútbol* soccer, and he closes his eyes as soon as the talking starts. "Hi, Papá," Vero tells him.

Nicky shuts himself in his room and does not come out when dinner is ready. Their mother pounds on his door, but he will not listen. A few hours later, he comes out dressed in ironed clothes, and their mother asks him where he is going on a Sunday night. He says, "To the drive-in," and outside, as if by magic, a whole carload of his friends from other towns rolls up to the front of the house. They honk once and he is gone.

When Vero and Nicky were much younger, their parents took them on Sunday drives. They went to mass in the morning because their father insisted, over to the old one-room church on Whittaker Street in the bad part of town. She remembers the church well, the long aisle and the faint outlines where old walls had been, separating the rooms of the old house the church used to be. It was either too hot or too cold, and after the service, their father would linger at the front door with other members, his shiny Chevy Impala at the curb with their mother inside, impatient. Vero and Nicky ran in the church's yard with the other children, panting with the effort and then waiting in line to drink from the outdoor fountain, an old porcelain basin with a small globe in the center where the water burbled up. The pipes ran along the outside walls, green with moss, rusty in other places, and always leaking—the church placed plywood over the soggy ground where the line to get a drink would form. And Vero would take her time, lowering her head like the old black woman had done in the afternoon movie on TV, an old black woman quivering in her step as a crowd gathered to watch her take a sip of water. Vero would take her sip like that, like everyone was watching her on Sunday, as if water never tasted so good.

Afterward, they went home to change clothes. They put on softer shoes, and she and Nicky brought playing cards and marbles and dolls for the backseat. Their father drove the perfectly conditioned Chevy Impala with its whole bench seat in the front and controls on the side that moved the whole thing forward and only he was allowed to touch them. Their father wore clean white T-shirts, and Vero remembers how massive and strong he looked and how their mother stretched her arm across the wide bench seat to hold his right shoulder while they drove. Their parents spoke to each other in soft Spanish as Vero and Nicky played in the backseat, the orchards rolling by. They always headed east to the Sierra Nevada, where the orange groves started to slant on the foothill slopes, and their mother would say, "Look, kids," to stop them from their playing. The Valley would give way in front of them: the flat ground surrendering to the big, sudden hills with tight rocks jutting out of the grass, the roads winding and curving. Vero and Nicky were the ones to say, "Look, look," because they could see out of the back window, at the Valley floor beginning to broaden, so wide. Their father drove carefully, the road twisting and their mother holding their father's thick shoulder, but their parents kept talking about whatever things they had been talking about. They climbed up, up, up, until their ears popped and then finally stopped at Kings Canyon National Park where there were wooden tables, and they got out and ate everything their mother had quietly stored in the trunk of the car while they had been changing out of their church clothes—the homemade burritos, the chips and salad, the cookies and Coke. They ate together at the tables beneath the giant mountain trees, their father smiling, their mother's gold hoop earrings swaying a bit when she leaned to kiss him.

Vero has forgiven her younger brother for stealing Julián, though she does not think that Julián was worth fighting for anyway, was not worth any humiliation. He had taken her into the backyard at the party and, against the fence, had put one, then two fingers in her, and she had let him. But so had another girl, one in Porterville, who her friends said did more than two fingers and ended up pregnant with his baby. She does not want Julián's baby. Nicky does not have to worry about having any babies—catching something, maybe. There are plenty of men, Vero knows, even in a small town like this, and the possibility of having a man with a wedding band no longer seems sinful to her. She notices how all the men, band or no band, look at her in the auto parts store, at the car she drives, at her own unadorned hands. She has grown accepting of all the possible ways of getting what she needs, daydreaming at the counter of the store, the cool chemical smell sometimes making her woozy.

Vero remembers how Julián came on the inside of her thigh: he pushed at her so he could rub himself clean on her skin. She forgives her younger brother because the whole experience with Julián was nothing to remember really, and she pities him for believing that someone like Julián is worth loving, that her little brother mistakes actions for affection. Vero wonders what goes through his mind when he steals the greeting cards, when he thinks of what to write in them. Sometimes she can't help thinking about what Julián and her younger brother did at the drive-in. She is ashamed to think of Julián coming on the inside of her younger brother's thigh. She is embarrassed to think of one, then two fingers.

Though Vero is not the one who is waiting for Sunday, the rest of the week is interminable. Nicky slouches. He slinks through the days, doesn't eat. Their parents grow more restless with each other, their father turning the volume up on the television, sometimes giving up altogether and going outside to the front lawn to stare at nothing. Though their father does not want to hear bickering, silence bothers him, too.

Their mother senses something amiss, and Vero knows, after a matter of days, that their mother has figured out what has happened. She does not know that Julián is locked up in the detention facility, but she has finally noticed his absence. She stops pestering Vero on Thursday morning.

On Sunday, everyone is silent. Their mother has made fried potatoes and eggs and fresh tortillas. They all eat separately, except Vero and Nicky. Nicky eats standing up, and he is ready to go by eleven. Under his shirt, Vero can see where he has tucked another little stack of cards in the waist of his pants.

She drives Nicky to buy a bucket of chicken, to the market to buy rolls and soda. The Macy's bag waits in his lap. About to suggest that they buy something different for the week, Vero realizes that perhaps Julián has asked for his favorite foods. It is not something Julián ever shared with her.

The sky is clear and blue, and the crop dusters on the old airfield are running at an oddly vigorous pace. When Vero pulls into the parking lot, she cannot hear the tires of the car rumble against the gravel underneath them. They stop the car in the middle of all the noise in the air, and Nicky does not hear her when she asks if he has everything.

The guard recognizes them but dutifully searches the Macy's shopping bag. She wants to tell Nicky to stop looking impatient and petty, because the older man takes more time on the letters, his thumb and forefingers along the envelopes. When he is done feeling them, he orders the cards opened, strict in his protocol. Vero thinks that he is an old man on a county work program, eager to follow rules, the paycheck important if not essential to his living. He reports everything, and he looks at Nicky much longer than he did last week.

From the bag, with Nicky surprised that he pulled it out, the older man fishes forth a little blue velvet box. He opens it as Vero watches, wondering what it is. She can see a gold cross and a chain, the older man's fingers fumbling through the padding, searching.

"Nicky," she says under her breath as they make their way to the picnic tables. "What is that? Where did you get that?"

"I bought it," Nicky answers, his voice as low as hers.

Julián is there to greet them, seated at a picnic table in a corner of the courtyard, and he does not get up when they approach. Nicky is awkward with his shopping bag and his half-stretched arms trying to encourage a hug, but Vero takes the bag from him to bring out the food. "Let's eat," she says.

When all the food is out, Julián moves to fold the bag but cannot because Vero has not removed the cards or the gift. He peeks into the bag and then, under his breath, says, "Nicky, no more cards. Okay?"

Nicky's face stiffens. "Why? Why no more cards?"

"Just don't bring them anymore," Julián answers, busying himself with the food. "I can't have them around."

"Are they not letting you keep them?" Nicky asks. "Where are the ones I gave you?"

"Jesus," says Julián. "Vero . . . ," he says, without any hesitation. Without any shame, Vero thinks, in asking to stop the beginnings of a quarrel.

Around them, Vero notices that the men in gray-green shirts are keeping an eye on them. The talk around the families jumps and starts, it seems to Vero, because mothers and girlfriends stop their week's stories to find out if the men are actually paying attention to them. She thinks she sees the men in gray-green shirts looking over the shoulders of their families.

She wants the visitation time to pass quickly. If they are watching Nicky, they are seeing him eat the fried chicken and separating the skin and bones. They are seeing him cast eyes at Julián, his mouth moving quickly because he is telling him something. They are seeing Julián pay too much attention to Nicky and not her. They are seeing that Nicky is not Julián's little brother. They are not seeing that she is the woman at the table. They are not seeing her mother—

imposing but pretty. They are not suspecting that she and Julián were the first ones to be involved with each other. She thinks the men are looking with disbelief at Nicky: that this must be the one who has written the letters, that the cards got away from Julián's possession in some way.

"Nicky," she says. "Please," she tells him, though he is saying nothing wrong.

"What?" he asks her. There is that petulance in his voice that their parents hate, and though no one is turning around just yet, Vero knows that a commotion is the last thing any of them wants. She wants to tell Nicky to tone everything down, that these men are capable of repeating what was done to him in the alley when he turned sixteen. But then she wonders if it is Nicky she wants to save from sadness, if she cares or not about Julián once he goes back inside. She wants to tell Nicky that this kind of anguish is for when you're married, when you are older and it means much more to lose someone. She thinks she is too young to know any of this but she does, because of the young girls all around them, because their mother and their father don't talk anymore and she does not want to be like them.

"Let's just finish up," Vero says, and Julián goes right on eating. He eats in big bites and hurriedly, but she can tell it isn't out of hunger.

They do not speak for the rest of the visitation, drain every last drop of the lukewarm soda, eat all the food, clear the table together. A little girl from one of the other families stumbles over to their table, her tiny shorts plump around the bottom from her diaper, and one of the young mothers runs to get her. She looks at Nicky.

When they rise to leave, Vero says, "I'll wait for you in the car," because she knows Nicky has been itching for an appropriate close. She wants to tell him not to do it, but she moves on to the exit. It is not her choice, not her life. She hurries quickly to the parking lot, nodding at the old guard, who nods back as if he sympathizes.

Nicky is crying on the way back, the Macy's bag folded and tucked under his arm. As he is approaching the car, she knows he is on the verge of believing he will fall apart and not piece himself together. He wants the turmoil. It is not the time to tell him she knows that he stole the necklace. It is not the time to tell him that this is not love, that he should not have tried to put the necklace on Julián in front of all of those people. He will learn on his own and maybe Julián will, too.

"Ready?" she says when he gets in. "We can go to the mall again. I'll pay for dinner later," she says, pulling out of the parking lot. Nicky looks out the window as they leave the facility, cries some more, and then leans back into his seat.

She holds hope for Nicky: she wants Nicky to be his own man. She wonders what got beat out of him; they kicked something out of him in the alley and something else has replaced it. He's become a thief so he can wear nice shirts with a group of boys like him in Fresno. After a long time at the mall, she dropped him off for the evening at a coffee shop where many of them hang out smoking cigarettes and holding their right elbows as they blow smoke into the hot night air. They stand around and look pretty, and all of them are sixteen like her younger brother, teasing each other, acting like girls. The confident ones act like girls. They smooth their shirts and pants and take another drag from their cigarettes, their sculpted hair glimmering in the coffee shop light.

Tonight, she has circled Shaw Avenue and Blackstone to clear her head and is now driving by to pick up Nicky and he waves her on—he'll catch up to her in a few minutes—and she goes to park the car. She's been in the coffee shop before, going in to get him because he has taken too long. The shop is comfortable chairs and ashtrays, skinny girls behind the counter, even skinnier boys. On the walls are the angry hairdos of Joan Crawford and Bette Davis. Their names are fake-signed in the corners of these posters. On a bulletin board is a flurry of old movie stars and someone has scrawled, "You're only as good as yesterday."

Once again, Vero has to park and go inside to get him. On the bulletin board, she can see a crumpled and folded picture that she knows is from the bookshop because of Nicky's pretty writing. "I wish I was Kim Hunter tonight!" he has written, on a picture of a bare-chested Marlon Brando. She wonders if any of them give a damn about these old stars or if they just think they should. In the group of boys, Nicky is laughing and joking, his arms loose and fingers splayed as if he is showing them rings. He is beautiful to look at, and Vero can see what Julián must be drawn by to behave the way he does in a town like theirs—her little brother holds so much promise in his fine bones, his beautiful hands, the way his face widens in a grin as he speaks in a place where he can feel like his true self, to boys his age who marvel at the picture he has shown them of his jailed boyfriend, the romance of so much trouble and muscle rolled up in one man who doesn't look like any of them. But Vero is not listening to what he is saying. She says, "Nicky, let's go," and he is so reluctant to pull away, and she wants to tell the rest of the boys in the shop—little mice, teeth, pretty clothes—to let him be his own man. Let him figure it all out for himself.

Nicky is going to cry again on the phone, Vero knows, because Julián has just called. Julián is telling Vero, "Find some way to tell him." He is telling her that they cannot come to visit on Sunday. She cannot listen to him: her own humiliation is not serving her well. This is the man who came on her leg and has done the same to her younger brother. This is the man who has done more than that and is not ashamed to speak with her. "Vero," he says, and his voice is shaking, "they cut my throat. They cut me and I have a scar all the way round my neck, Vero. Tell Nicky he can't come."

"God," she says to Julián and nothing else, because he is scared and what can she do.

Nicky comes into the living room when he hears her talking too softly. "Who's on the phone?"

"I have to go," she says, and hangs up quickly.

"Who was that?"

"None of your business," she says, but Nicky presses. He follows her into the kitchen.

"Was that Julián?"

She checks to make sure their mother is not around. "Sit down, Nicky."

"What for?"

"Because you need to sit down," Vero says, but she is worried that their mother will walk in, or their father, and there is no time to soften him. "We're not visiting Julián on Sunday."

"I knew it!" Nicky begins, but she stops him.

"Nicky, listen to me," she says. "Trust me . . . ," she tries.

He keeps at it. "Vero . . ."

"Your cards, Nicky. . . . You just can't do that kind of thing, don't you see?" she says, looking as hard as she can into her younger brother's eyes, because he is rushing into life too quickly and the tears that are forming are not of real hurt. Not yet. Nicky is not their mother. She looks as hard as she can into Nicky's eyes before he closes them to shed his tears and begin the whole storm of anger. He puts his head on the table, as if a few weeks is too much to bear, and she waits to tell him the details. He does not need the added drama of a gang of men with secret knives. He does not need to lie awake imagining Julián with his eyes peeled in the dark—she knows he will come out safe. She suspects that the cut throat is not as serious as it sounds, that it is a scare and nothing more, that the young men in the gray-green uniforms already resent being in a low-security barracks and know that life at a real prison is not worth the deepening of whatever sharp object they held to Julián's neck. She remembers the old guard thumbing the envelopes and his strict vision, and she reasons that the cut on the throat is made with something sharp but ultimately benign. A scrap of aluminum can, a filed rusty screw extracted from a bedpost, a thin razor tucked under the tongue of one of those Ivanhoe girls rocking a two-month-old baby.

"Vero," their mother tells her one night in the living room. "Is Nicky taking drugs?"

Their father tells them to be quiet and turns up the volume on the television.

"He's sleeping all the time, he doesn't come out of his room, he's not eating."

"I don't think there's anything to worry about," Vero says, and in the light of the television set, she tries her best not to look back at her mother, who must be feeling foolish. Her mother must know that something more than drugs would keep away sleep and hunger. Vero thinks they both remember how their mother behaved years and years ago, when their father changed from being the man with the big shoulders and the shiny car. There was anger between them. He left, and their aunt had to care for them because their mother slept all through those days and did not eat. After their father returned, he had insisted on quiet. Since then, it has been so, all of these years.

"I'm just so worried," their mother says, but her voice doesn't convince Vero. She thinks their mother only wants to sound worried, because they both know that soon enough Nicky will be leaving the house again, gone until the beginning of the next day.

Several weeks later, she drives Nicky to the detention facility, and she expects to see Julián standing in the parking lot with a plastic bag of clothes, but no. They park the car and go to the main office where Julián waits for thin yellow papers. He is issued a little sack containing his wallet and his car keys and even the old tissues that had been in his pockets, and he is asked to confirm that everything is in order. He is wearing the brown khakis and the white muscle shirt that he came in with, his dark hair thick and in need of a cut. Vero sees his neck: just as he told her, he has a thin purple line looped around his neck, a permanent deep mark. Nicky is looking at him, too, and she tries to see if he is looking at the purple scar or at the gold cross and chain that doubles over it. The chain hides the scar and draws attention to it at the same time.

Maybe because Nicky knows better, there are no words between them in the lobby, only Julián putting down the pen and receiving his thin yellow papers. He says to them, "Ready?" with a small smile on his face. He is sporting a goatee, thick and unruly, and he has lost weight from the bad food.

They exit, passing a young woman with a child in tow; she rushes in anticipation. It is her day to see whoever is inside get out. Her black hair is done up. Nicky looks at her and his face holds a slight grin, and Vero cannot say if he is making fun of her or not.

In the car, Nicky turns his whole body around to speak to Julián, beaming the entire time. A crop duster flies directly over the road as they are leaving, descending onto the old airfield, Vero slowing down as if the plane were about to clip the top of their car.

"It's nothing," Nicky says, turning to look, but keeping his body turned backward, Julián finally out. "It's nothing."

"So how's it feel?" Vero offers.

"Good," Julián says, matter-of-factly.

"You wore my necklace," Nicky says, and Vero looks at Julián in the rearview mirror. He is staring at her younger brother with a sad smile, and she can see the beginnings of the scar descending into him, into the space where the mirror can no longer show him. There is so much she wants to say to both of them now—that this will be the last time she will do this much for her little brother; that Nicky will finally see what kind of man Julián really is; that this happiness her little brother feels should be reserved for someone who wants more than just his pretty looks. She wants to tell Nicky that he is as pitiful as the young woman with the baby in tow that they just saw. *There will be better than this,* she wants to say to Nicky, *someone to treat you right,* but they are driving through the empty fields six miles from their small town and that kind of love might not be here for him.

She looks long at the deep mark on Julián's neck and sees herself running her finger across it, the way she knows Nicky will do later. Vero stares at him too long, drifting, and the car dips briefly into the slant of the shoulder, but she corrects quickly. "Sorry," she apologizes as the car jostles a bit.

"Doesn't scare me," says Nicky.

After their meal under the trees of the national park, their mother and their father had climbed them back in the car and they started the descent into the Valley. The vehicles on the way up came so slowly, and their father zipped along the curves, hugging the car so tight against the walls of the mountains looming above them. Their mother clutched his shoulder and told him to slow down, but her voice was playful and enjoyed the thrill. On the one side, the proximity of the mountain wall. On the other, Vero and Nicky could see the steep drops on the sides of the road, a tumble of river canyon and thick trees. The car went faster and faster, their stomachs heavy with lunch, and their father laughed, lightly pressing the brakes, and told them that when they learned to drive, they should not wear out their brakes. They should coast. They should let things handle themselves and just stay in the lane and there would be nothing to be scared of. Their mother clutched his shoulder because she was afraid and because she loved him. Vero watched them. On her side of the car, the mountain wall was so close she thought she could roll down the window and scrape her knuckles; she flinched away from the window as if in pain. On the other side, at the drop into the canyons, Nicky hung close to the window to see into the deep and Vero reached over to lock the door because she did not want her little brother to fall out. They went faster, their father laughing, their mother loving him, Nicky peering out of the window, out at the edge.

Everything the White Boy Told You

Tell us, Celio, what the white boy told you that day. Celio at twenty-two with an unfortunate name, always the pause when you say it. Tell us what he told you, though we already know what he told you because he tells the same story to everyone, all of us—we've all met him. Tell us about the town in Maine where he grew up, the small town where it snows until April sometimes, flakes as late as May one year when he was six. You pictured leaves falling, didn't you—like us—leaves bright red, the way they gleam gold on calendars when you flip to October? Tell us about the family plot where he hopes to be buried someday, no matter who he winds up with, and how he looked at you when he said that. Did you feel the little pull of loss already beginning when he mentioned it? Tell us when exactly he mentioned the family grave—was it after the first drink or the second, or did he wait until you were out of the bar? Tell us if he asked anything about you, where you grew up in Texas—near Corpus Christi or up by Abilene?—and if it mattered to him, Texas geography and where your people are buried. We have our guesses.

Celio, we've been there, all of us, the befores, the way-back-whens. On the second visit to his apartment, the morning after while he made you coffee, he handed all of us (most of us) to you in that photo album. Didn't he? Ask yourself what he was asking you to see, the words came to you because you stared at him so long. Tap your index finger to your temple (the right one) and say, *You're getting in here.*

We want you to surprise him—sooner than later—to save you, Celio. Because he has told you all that he wants to tell you right now about Maine, about the family you will never meet, about the town you will never see. And he is afraid to ask about where you are from. We have told him things—about houses falling apart in Arizona, in California; about the rotted kitchen counters in a Brownsville apartment and how the snails appeared through the plumbing, the Morton salt canister by the sink; about how two nails and a piece of heavy string made for a lock in houses like ours; about the dog out back dragging a heavy chain around a lemon tree and made mean with a stick; about pink and aqua paint being the cheapest, but still the walls everywhere remained chipped; about the chalky film sticking in our throats from powdered milk; about men living twenty to a house on all corners of our neighborhoods, and that was normal; about our brothers' rooms out back, the window screens rusting and peeling and letting in the humid night air; about the aunt who made money by selling dolls, crocheted dresses with hidden Coke cans serving as the torsos; about the ninety-dollar encyclopedias our mothers bought for nothing, the roaches trapped between the pages; about tea when we were hungry; about lice outbreaks at school two times a year, guaranteed; about how the boys in town still grew impossibly muscular through all of this and we couldn't have them; about the guilt of having cousins who still live like this in Colorado, in New Mexico; about how we would never go back.

Tell him, Celio, like we told him. Maybe you're the one. Maybe he will not stop telling you the things he is telling you. Maybe he will not mention one of us to you, how you remind him of one of us, how it is too painful for things to go any further. He will tell you this anyway, sooner or later, because he is *not at that point in my life right now.* So get in his head, Celio. At least for us. Give us something about Corpus Christi or Abilene or wherever you are from. Give us something about where you think you are headed. We're all in it—tell him so that he has the whole story, so many pieces—and he will come back to one of us. Because it happens, how we all revisit what we've done and been. He is going to look back and reconsider someday, and he will have some of the story straight if you do your part. We're sure of it! Do it, Celio. Give it all up to him, like we did. Tell him your whole story and see which one of us he comes back to.

THE HARBOR OF HANDS

Hombres

On any night, men flit down Forty-second Street, or Seventeenth, or
Broadway. There's not much to tell about them except they whistle
Sondheim, they hum. They wear shirts that are not just white shirts,
but Italian and expensive to the cuff. They walk as if they belong in
any part of the city, as if city is what they have always known.

There are men who sit in cafés and split pastries among themselves.
They share frugal bits of chocolate cake with silver forks, twirling
their fingers as they bite. Their hands are manicured; they have held
telephones all day.

The cafés are kind places. It is all soft backlighting, bulbs camou-
flaged by plants, lowered lamps that don't create harsh shadows, urging them to flirt. In this light, it is safe to tease with the brown boy in a
too-tight apron. It is safe to look at him and see that he is thin waisted,
and he reminds some of them of vases they own, with necks for only
one stem.

The cafés are the kind of places where one of these men will step
away from the rest, if encouraged to do more than look. After asking
if his shirt is Italian and only once worn, it takes such little work to
get his story started. First, the small town in rural New York, how
his parents did not love him—but his uncle did; there's the story of a
robbery in a French train station, all the money gone, but the adven-

ture of sleeping on the benches; that guitars and opera mean something, how he still clutches his guitar after he's finished singing to himself; or, at age ten, how he sang opera in his father's ear.

I can't explain the men in the city who lived in rural towns and now seek out Italian shirts. I can't explain the ones who stroke the softness of the cloth and ask me to do the same, before they tell me of the same father and uncle, the fists and the adolescence. But I envy the way in which the skyscrapers and the street bustle convinces their tone, that they speak like no one has stories and everyone should listen.

I watch how, bit by bit, it is their hands that become important, how they hold or push away. Later, in the dark of their bedrooms, it is the faint glow of their fingers moving in the air above us, how they keep asking for attention. Or the blue tint of veins as their arms stretch across the pillows, the tip of each finger counting another thing to say to fill the dark. It is city lights that does it to them, these rural boys in New York, a panic that comes from a fear of waking up again, predawn on a sleepy farm. To the kind of cold they don't remember, the kind that makes them light-headed.

Like the brown boy in the café wearing the apron, I cannot explain them. That boy will tell you about ships and crossing water, about babies and southern seas. That boy, I can tell by the way he never answers them, knows that telling stories never settles scores. He serves them chocolate cake and strudel but doesn't explain hunger, that it isn't frustration in a small-town bed. He pours coffee, says nothing of places where uncles are the least of worries.

Skyshot

I tell my friend Quetz, "Count as soon as the screen lights up. See how far you can get."

Sometimes we're lucky. Quetz says, "Music doesn't matter, does it?" and I shake my head no, waiting for voices. We can count to twenty or thirty when it's a movie we like. Even Quetz says, "It's too easy to have someone speak." Even Quetz says that.

I say, "I don't like voices in the dark, and then the face showing up."

Neither does Quetz. "The voice never matches the face. It's disappointing."

We've come to like: orchestrations by Miklos Rozsa; inventive title designs, like the office building and the arrows in *North by Northwest;* what we think are Joan Crawford's legs turning at the carport gate. Quetz detests bland landscape shots and credits typed over open fields. I hate John Williams.

What's best are the aerial shots, even the sloppy ones from helicopters and their dragonfly shadows skimming along the terrain. We like the way that the camera descends from nowhere like a sudden cloud. Everywhere below is just rigid lines and intersections until the camera gets closer and closer, or the scene clips to the real story, and all that geometry suddenly means something.

So how to begin this, without a camera? Just yesterday I was flying back home after seeing my mom in L.A. and all below me was the giant square of Fresno. And all around it more squares—orchards and vineyards and farmers' cattle grounds. How to begin a story out of this mess of order? (Quetz and I have been taking classes at Fresno State from an old crudgy professor. Abstract art. He says a couple things about the impossibilities of geometry. He says, Geometry, not figures. He says, Shapes, not stories. And then he looks blankly at all of us when we stare back.)

I flew in yesterday and saw where I lived. I want to be able to say that it's like the Robert Altman movie I rented where an army of helicopters is spraying for Medflies over L.A. It made L.A. seem dangerous, contaminated. But L.A. is where a lot of us say we will go someday, four hours south of the Central Valley, crossing the Grapevine on I-5 and descending straight into a city of limousines and lights. In winter, when the entire floor of the Valley is shrouded in the thickest fog, only the rising of the freeway breaks through into the mountains, and then suddenly Los Angeles and you're reminded that there's sun after all.

From way up, even in my descending plane, I would have never guessed that the trees hide things. Small things: Robert Altman didn't show the tiny triangular fly traps put out by the farmers. But we have traps here and the farmers look at them, sometimes with a local television crew filming as they open a triangle and see if a black speck is stuck to the lining. We've been lucky. None of them has been trapped here.

Quetz is in his twenties just like me. We go to school together. Each semester, we look over the class schedules for Fresno State and try to arrange our courses so we can save on gas. Sometimes it works, sometimes it doesn't. He took the course on abstract art just for the hell of it, so he could keep his financial aid for the semester. He's a mechanic, and when his technical classes cancel out on him, he sits next to me and wonders what the hell he's doing. I write his essays for him.

Quetz is one of those kids whose parents were hung up on Chicano nationalism back in the sixties and named their children after Aztec gods. Quetz spells his name Quetzalcoatl, but he freely tells me, "I've never been able to say it and I don't give a shit either." He's been wanting to leave our town for years now and he thinks he's missed his chance. I say, "We can leave once we get our degrees," and he turns to me without saying anything and I know what he wants to tell me: What will we do in Los Angeles with these kids from UCLA and USC and the ones who've come down from Stanford?

He is not rational: when I remind him he can work as a mechanic, he says no way and then he says, out of the blue, "You know, L.A. is nothing but cars," and in the same spirit, he believes I can pick up my own love by simply moving to Hollywood. "You can break into movies," he tells me.

I ignore him. Quetz suggests this because I make him spend so much time watching movies with me, and he sits still even through the ones he doesn't like. We know Robert Altman because no one rents his movies in our town and so he gets onto the ninety-nine-cent shelf along with the old videotapes from before 1980—the big bulky boxes with curling cellophane covers. We discovered Hal Ashby this way and Sidney Lumet. Quetz likes William Friedkin and I liked Martin Ritt best, until I saw Altman.

At the end of *Nashville,* Quetz says, "You don't even like country music," but I tell him that I really liked it, that it wasn't like any of the movies we had seen before.

"No," he says. "How come all those people don't know each other after three hours?" and I shake my head at him because I don't know, either.

I tell him: People and city, how they make up a city. But he doesn't go for it. He says to me, "They didn't talk to each other and they kept talking at the same time," and he shakes his head as he lights up a joint.

Sometimes I'll have the joint with him and sometimes not. This time I do because he says, "So no more Martin Ritt, huh?" and his tone implies that I don't care anymore about how Sally Field reminded us of the people at the tomato-packing plant on our side of town.

"I liked *Nashville*," I say again.

He tries, "I think people should talk to each other in movies, and that's it," and he moves over to where I am sitting on my couch. Before I know it, he's kissing me, the both of us in my living room, and I don't worry that my father will walk in. I used to, but I don't anymore, because it doesn't matter. What consequences, when nothing matters in a town this small, if you leave.

I wish I could say this takes place over five days in this little town, and there will be this many people who are part of my story, and this many of them matter. But I can't, because me and Quetz and my father and Quetz's parents and Mrs. Santos are all scattered. I wish I could sit the way my aunts do at the kitchen table and tell my father, This is why I'm leaving. But I don't know how to put it together and I wish everything important in my life had happened in just the past five days, so it would be fresh. And all I would have to do would be to say, Here, this is why this means this and that means that. Because it all happened so close together, and time, at least, can help me close the distances.

My mother left. She is in Los Angeles without my father, and I have stayed with him because, behind his olive and beige clothes—shirts and pants and shorts (my father is no longer in the military after thirty years)—my father is alone. I see now that he wants to look fresh out of the army, wearing white T-shirts sometimes. He wants to look strong but is angry and hurt whenever I travel to see my mother. He is either angry or not angry.

"Come here," my father said one day. He was standing at our living room window, which faces the street, the curtains pulled back because it was late afternoon and the sun didn't hit that side of the house. "Look," he said, with a faint gesture toward the shady street.

I got up from watching a movie and walked over. "What?" I asked, and looked out, seeing only an older neighbor as she slowly walked along. In the late afternoons and early evenings, as long as it was warm out, she circled the block to get her exercise.

"What about her?" I asked my father.

"You notice how she never looked up in this direction?"

"Yeah."

"And we have this big window."

"What about it?" I asked him as she left our sight.

He said bluntly, "When her husband wasn't around. Mrs. Santos. I had an affair with that woman."

"Mrs. Santos? When?"

"When her husband went to Texas for a month. His little brother got killed in Vietnam and they shipped him back to San Antonio for burial."

I didn't say much because I wanted to do the math—maybe twenty-five years, when my father was my age, in his twenties. And that woman, maybe forty or so.

My father looked up at me. He was wearing his olive shorts and was barefoot, and this made me think that he'd been on his way out to water the grass and then stopped. I thought if someone had been looking through the window at us, staring at each other, they would have known exactly what was happening and what the problem was: he was on the verge of telling me and I was on the verge of asking. If someone had been looking through that window, they might have shouted to us to speak.

Mrs. Santos came down the block while the two of us continued standing by the window, and she passed by without making a twitch toward the house. My father stopped watching me.

"It's always been like that. She went her way. I went mine."

Lily Tomlin plays a wife and she goes to a barbecue or a fund-raiser and she sits talking to a woman, the way my aunts do, telling stories, telling them well. She never gets to the whole story, and I never know why she's telling it in the first place. She circles around a motorcycle accident and a woman with a bump on her head. There are mentions of motorcycles and beautiful boys, how she walked into a whole ward full of them and every single one was paralyzed.

I think another director would have shown that ward—I know I would have—because it made me sad to think of so many clean beds and legs wrapped in casts and boys with shaved heads to make way for stitches. What Lily Tomlin said had nothing to do with anything, but the way she told it, the way my aunts tell stories—something matters even when the pieces don't quite fit. I couldn't stop thinking of a whole hospital floor of beautiful boys, all of them mangled, and what they might have done to deserve such a fate.

Time seems like it's running out on me and Quetz, and yet we don't know what to compare it against. There is only now. This is August and our registration dates for Fresno State have come and gone, neither of us with classes, and now we are broke.

We sit in the bakery in the middle of downtown, splitting a whole lunch between us. Quetz takes a bite of his sandwich and I can't help but think about the money he is swallowing. I can tell he's not thinking right.

He says, "Let's just go to L.A. Tomorrow."

I stare out the window because it does not feel immediate. It does not feel like a tension. There is nowhere to work; I haven't told my father that we screwed up registration for school and my money is gone. What would change about home, me always watching movies and us not talking?

"My dad," I tell Quetz. "I can't leave my dad," but can't say why.

Quetz scoffs, pushes his plate away. He is clearing the space between us. He says, "Give me your hand," and he stretches his arm on the table, reaching for me.

I look at him. He isn't fearful.

"Just hold my hand," he insists.

Ned Beatty is wearing a tight brown polyester shirt. He is wearing it the way only Ned Beatty can. It's beige rather than brown. He is listening. He is playing a man who is able to listen, but doesn't, not when his deaf son signs to him. His son tries to tell him a simple story about swimming, about diving to the bottom of the pool, touching that space. It's hard to figure out exactly what his son is saying, but it's easy at the same time. It's easy to see he's talking about going down, and then farther down. He even breaks it down, to the individual letters, his fingers quick. That's all he wants: to tell his father about touching bottom. But Ned Beatty doesn't listen.

The last conversation I had with my father before I left was about Altman. While I was watching *Nashville* for the second time, my father came into the room. He said, though he spoke perfectly good English, "I hate movies that aren't in Spanish" as he picked up the box.

"Altman—that's German, right? Like *alemán*? That's 'German' in Spanish," and before I knew it he started explaining the German-Mexican alliances during the wars and how Mexico would have been screwed if they followed through with anything. "Do you know a German offered your grandpa money to blow up buildings in Los Angeles?" he asked.

"The movie's almost over," I told him, and he watched with me as Ronee Blakley sang a song about Idaho, an enormous American flag fluttering across the screen.

"Look at Argentina," my father said suddenly. "And Uruguay. Where are they now, for helping out those fuckers?" I nodded my head, my father stepping outside to water the lawn in his olive shorts and bare feet, and I had absolutely no idea what he was angry about.

I'll say one good thing about that art professor—at least he taught me to study things. Since I've been shelling out my spare change for cheap movies, I've been ignoring the plots and the stars and the music and noticing how the director looks at things. Robert Altman does it best, I think. He likes to look at people and likes you to do the same and make some judgments about them—why they do things, like the waitress who can't sing.

I like those moments when the camera sneaks up on someone. Or, it's just two people talking, and then suddenly you notice that the camera is moving closer and closer and closer until it's right on one person's face and suddenly everything that person says could be terrible and devastating. It is just that person's face, the roundness of the cheekbones and the eyes knowing that what happens next could make a horrific kind of difference. It means listening very hard.

I am not naive. From the supermarket, my father brings home tabloid magazines, and these same faces are in fancy clothes and dark ties. I like to think that Robert Altman is not like them, that he sits at a park bench or an airport lounge and waits for people to walk by with their lives impossible to hide. Or that Sidney Lumet walks the streets of New York trying to memorize every stretch of sidewalk. I know that Martin Ritt doesn't think about how Melvyn Douglas has to kill all his cattle and be left with nothing, or how Patricia Neal would be one of the few people to run away from Paul Newman. He doesn't sit there and cry into his hands. But I like to think that he does.

The first time I ever really looked at Quetz was at the Sunflower Festival in our town a couple of days ago, a whole bevy of queens and princesses selling raffle tickets downtown or at the supermarket, trying to win a crown. We have a large park in the center of our town, the tallest trees around, and they gave us shade all day as we mingled around the amphitheater and the food booths.

It was at night that I first looked at him, during the intermission for the beauty pageant. We were on the Ferris wheel, a rickety and groaning one, moving up into the dark. Below us, a line of couples inched along the gate, watching. I let my legs dangle, spread open, my wrists hanging over the safety bar with as much nonchalance as I could give.

Quetz didn't seem to care. He let his leg touch mine, and he didn't laugh and point out at anything, the way some people did. On our way up, he said nothing and stared straight ahead to the darker out-skirts of town, visible past the yellow lights and blue neon of the festival. He looked at the fields he had to work in as a kid and how these people did all the harvesting and then came here to spend their money.

Down below, a whole group of girls ran dizzy, cotton candy in their hands—they were rushing to catch their friends in the pageant who could dance or sing. Each one of them seemed pretty as they raced by.

"Hey," Quetz said to me, and I braced myself for him to say some-thing too loudly with these people watching us, our legs touching in the dark. "What are we waiting for?" he asked.

On the stage, we could see (and then hear) a *ranchera* being sung by a tiny girl in a green dress. The sequins caught the light of camera bulbs and twinkled at us. I didn't know what Quetz was asking me, so I listened to the tiny girl and the way the audience applauded her.

I was afraid Quetz would turn to me and say, "I love you," that he wouldn't care about being in a public park with so many people around. That he would hand the ride operator a twenty-dollar bill and tell him, "Keep us spinning," until the carnival had to pack its tents and the soothsayers went home.

He did not continue, would not explain. I think he was looking at the horizon as if Los Angeles were that close. I saw his eyes tense, his mouth narrow against what occupied him. He was angry, though I still don't know about what, and he made me think of my father—

how so many people here behave the same way. They say things and don't finish, maybe because they don't know what comes next.

Right then, I wished I had a camera. I wished I had it so Quetz could see, somehow, his face in profile and how his anger came across even though he didn't mean it. There, closer, and closer, until the sheer proximity made him act and say, "It's this town, don't you see?" Or, "I need out." Or, "Why don't you come with me?"

They were crowning a winner down below, and the crowd applauded on command when the master of ceremonies came forward and told them, *"Un fuerte aplauso por estas muñecas, por favor."* They proclaimed the tiny girl in the green dress the winner. Her face, even from where we sat on the Ferris wheel, broke into a grin as bright as any of the lights at the carnival.

"That country music movie we watched the other day," Quetz said, "didn't it end with someone getting shot? That's what this needs."

"Quetz, that's a shitty thing to say," I told him. Though I pictured him doing it, I know he would never do such a thing. He was just being mean. In the movie, it was a way to end things. I knew Quetz could do more than just end things.

Shelley Duvall is a bad niece and walks around Nashville in wigs and tight shorts and even changes her name. She fucks every man in the movie, just about, and it doesn't matter that she's skinny and looks ridiculous. You have to wonder what makes someone do that. Why she's a niece and not a daughter, and why it's only about her shallowness. She never gets to speak, never gets to say, only her uncle running after her, desperate for some explanation about why she missed her aunt's funeral. She never gets to say.

What to make of Quetz's room: a tiny shed of planks in the backyard of his cousin's house. What to think of how I went over there in broad daylight and shut the door behind me. Or, in the cold of winter, how we piled blankets onto his slender bed and camped out there, smoking pot. I think, because he is not afraid, that I have become too brazen, that I'm forgetting how small this town is, that we're old enough to know what we're doing.

Quetz isn't afraid: not of what we're doing, not of his parents, not of the cold. I admire him.

His parents know. I sometimes run into them at the grocery store or buying Mexican bread at the bakery. They put their money down angrily.

I wonder if my father ever runs into them. He used to be good friends with them; so did my mother. But my father never mentions a word.

"Just hold my hand," Quetz insists, and he keeps his arm stretched on the table, reaching for me and he is not afraid.

I tell him, "I wish I had a camera," and I know he's thinking a Kodak, a throwaway roll of film. But I want a real camera, one that could circle around us. How else to describe the rush inside of me, the questions that don't matter anymore—telling my father that I want to leave and how he'll react, if my mother will take me in. The exhilaration of the moment is what is most important, and I want to see my own face. I close my eyes to see it, from far away and then closer, how I must look, Quetz waiting for me to say yes.

The people around us don't matter anymore. And we don't know where we're going in L.A. or how. So it is our hands—as if a camera really were above us—the space Quetz cleared on the table. It is, for now, just our hands clasped, the spoons and the lips of the round coffee cups, the mismatched butter knives. There are two plates and the half-finished sandwiches.

What Altman did at the end of *Nashville* was right on the money: if you look up at the sky in the middle of the afternoon, it isn't blue. It isn't a happy ending. It washes out with the terrible brightness of the sun. I look out the bakery window, my decision made to go to L.A., holding Quetz's hand, and I can hear people clearing their throats.

SKYSHOT

But what's behind all of this is not the leaving. Or the things making me go. I cannot explain, the way movies can with their happy endings. This is not a happy ending just because of our clasped hands. When I look up at the sky, it hurts, but rather than close my eyes to fade it out, I come back down to the street. My town's main street. It doesn't look cramped anymore. I don't want it to look that way. I want the looking up, the open space sudden, mine.

Teatro Japonés

I

You saw him in a coffee shop where you can look, where all the men sit with their legs crossed just so. He had blond hair that was pulled back in a ponytail and you thought, if you had seen him from behind, you would have said *girl,* because his back was so narrow and thin.

But he was a boy, all right, and reading—a real book—not flipping through a magazine for furniture, but a book about Japanese theater, in Spanish no less. TEATRO JAPONÉS, in gold letters, his fingers hiding the rest of the title. He never looked up, so you watched him, and his lips moved when he read, and you lost yourself remembering church as a six-year-old, the elderly man who read along with the Bible passages, you sleeping under the pews.

II

You've been teaching the Costa Rican boy how to read, and he draws pictures for you. Frogs and goats because he's practicing spelling and the letter *g.* He has the *guh* down. *Fro—guh,* he tells you. *Guh. Guh-irl.* He fumbles all over the softer sound. *Juh. Juh. Giraffe,* you tell him, but he can only draw a picture, so you move on, because you can't think of other words at the moment. But on the train ride home, the Costa Rican boy's little voice comes back to you to say words he can't know how to use. He says to you, riding on the train, *Gesture. Gentleman.*

III

You can't pronounce his name, for the life of you, you can't, even though it's Spanish. He says no one can, so he goes by Allan, and you talk with him some more against the loud, loud backdrop of the club and you can't hear him, his voice slipping, his drink losing to the ground. You don't think you're hearing him right, and you swear he has a lisp, and you feel terrible for thinking so, because he's that kind of boy, and you don't like it when people think all boys have lisps. But you have to bend your head to hear him, and it isn't the rum and Coke but his tongue and the roof of his mouth, and the boy sees you trying to listen carefully and looks you in the eye, and you understand why he makes himself as pretty as he looks, prettier than anyone in the entire room.

IV

The boy with the blond ponytail left his book on the table, upturned, to go the bathroom, and you had the chance to flip through the book and see if it really was Spanish and how complicated. You thought to yourself that you would ask him, but when he came back, he was smoothing the ponytail and tucking it under the nape of his collar, putting on his coat, so you would never do more than smile and wonder what he would have told you about first, if you asked him any question you wanted. Who taught him how to read, put his fingers to the page, and showed him? Who sounded his lips? You wondered how long his hair had been that way—all his life?—and did he run away from his mother's kitchen like the kids in your town, when the scissors at home meant no money for the barber. Or were you really waiting for what he sounded like—not really paying attention to what he would say—but what he sounded like. To say, he sounds like a boy. A pretty boy, no less.

Monkey, *Sí*

I

First, there was George (really Jorge) and Pedro and Eddie. Two Jims. Mark, Philip, and Andrew. Greg, Jeff, Joe, and John. Vinny, from Baltimore. David, Tyler (Chinese American and beautiful), Carlos, Pablo, Wilson, Oscar, *y* Roberto (the only real Spanish speakers: *¡Niño! ¡Nene! ¡Mono!*). How to translate their affections? Child. Baby. Monkey. *Claro que sí.*

We will call this one Tomás, even though the white men try to call him Tommy (and he hates it in two ways: the diminutive Bobbys and Dannys and Billys for men too old for names like that, the fact that these men can't say his name right). We will call him Tomás. They will say Tommy.

Someone else will call him Tomás: his name is Nestor, and he is in love with Tomás. Nestor is dark skinned and small and longs to be under Tomás, because he is tall, with arms that could shield him from the cold.

But it never gets cold here, because it is Fresno. Why Fresno? A good question, but others are already in line. And this roster of names—are these friends of Tomás? Tricks? A list of lovers that only shows how flighty a character Tomás will turn out to be? Do we already know that Nestor will lose out by the end of the story (and in life, because we have mentioned that he is dark skinned and small and these men don't like either)?

We will have to let the list go. We will not say anything about Tomás here. Or about why this is in Fresno and not San Francisco or New York or any other big American city where whole battalions of these men dress like nuns and nurses to rile the mayors. Not these men. Not here. And Nestor will come close to death, by his own doing, but we already know he'll survive it and live (unfortunately) in continued unhappiness. What has Tomás to do with any of this?

II

Nestor likes Tomás because of what he wears. He wears muscle shirts and open short-sleeves, unbuttoned, even to work, and Nestor thinks that no one complains because Tomás smiles with straight teeth and teases the women. All in good nature because Tomás has no hair on his chest breaking through the white cotton of his shirt, no gold chains (not even a thin one) to remind the women that he is as dark as the men they generally stay away from. Nestor likes Tomás because Tomás's mother knows what her son has done and wants to do, and none of it seems to faze her. Perhaps because she is younger than most mothers, still wears lipstick, and was glad to see her husband leave. She wears heels and holds Nestor's cheek to kiss him every time he comes to visit Tomás. She kisses him as if she knows what Nestor wants, as if to say, *This world isn't made for you. You don't want someone like me, and someone like my son doesn't want you.* She kisses him like that.

III

We can see them, from a distance, as a group of friends. We know that a group of friends walking together to the one bar in town cannot line up side by side as they do on television. They must walk in pairs or threes, sometimes ones. From a distance, we can see them as just a group of friends, but if we got closer, if we let the adjectives take on their clothes (black pants, loose blue jeans, shiny shoes, shirts spread across impossible backs) or scents in the air (cigarettes because some of them get nervous, the mingle of three colognes, one like lemons), we would find that the group is a mangle of hesitations. We can see two of them trying to walk on either side of Tomás, that Nestor is alone and trying to keep up.

Later, if we like, we can get as close to Nestor as we want when we listen to Tomás tell him about why the two were walking on either side of him. Nestor will be on the telephone. He will listen to Tomás as he tells him about all three of them occupied with each other. We can see what Tomás does to one of these men in particular, how the other sat back and watched in a green armchair in the corner, but it will be more telling to stay on Nestor, his hand on the receiver. He will be wearing a white T-shirt when he hears this and little jeans with the cuffs rolled up and no shoes. He will be pressing one hand against his forehead as he hears all of this. His heart will be beating fast and we will leave him alone to put down the receiver and do whatever he does when Tomás says these terrible things to him.

IV

On paydays from the ice company where he works, Nestor cashes his check at the draw window. We can see the Mexican nationals snicker at him, but Nestor cannot, because his back is turned and he is busy counting his week's pay in twenties. He double-counts always. We can see the way the men look at him because Nestor keeps his shirts tucked and his pants are snug and he stands on tiptoe at the window. All his posture suggests is what these men laugh at, but there's really no telling which of the men are just going along with the taunt (because Fresno is not a place to be that lonely).

Nestor with the tucked-in shirt and snug pants is going to San Francisco with Tomás. They will drive in Nestor's car, and Nestor will pay for the gas and for hamburgers along the side of Highway 99 when Tomás gets hungry. They are going for an overnight in the city, to dance in the Big City clubs, and drive home tired. Tomás is tired already, and when the boredom of the Valley gets to him (which is not very long—he is bored of his life), Nestor will keep driving. The roads are straight, so we will look at them, because Nestor is too busy stealing glances at Tomás's sharp cheekbones and his brown eyes swirling in sleep. We will have to keep a lookout for the many diesel trucks that are coming back empty from San Francisco and up north, coming to take away oranges and lemons and cotton, racing by because they are always late. Nestor will admire how Tomás slouches in the passenger seat with his legs spread wide the way so many men do, and he wants to see himself hover there. We will notice the approaching coastal range that fringes the western part of the Valley and how purple and green it is, a tip of fog already visible at its peak, and we will breathe in and try to feel exhilarated by this vision. We will try to match how Nestor feels driving Tomás in his car, sleeping as he is, wishing someone else were driving them so that he could nestle against him without Tomás ever waking up.

V

The list of names. Here are their problems.

One of them alerted his parents about his wet dream concerning the wrestling team. Another will bore us to tears if we listen too long about how his parents kicked him out of the house (he thinks he is the only one). Too many of them are alcoholics for anybody to take their pain seriously. One is a heavy drug user and is ashamed to admit it and the others too unaware to catch on. One was just visiting Fresno and ended up living there when he saw how cheap it was. One plays opera in the dark to go to sleep, very softly (because a man in Los Angeles told him he loved him and gave him the recordings). David and Tyler (the Chinese American boy, the beautiful one) and Pablo were all molested as children, repeatedly and terribly, but they will never talk about it. But we know about it, because something must come after them besides adjectives. Tyler is more than Chinese American and beautiful: he is a singer and has charmed several other young men into him by singing in their ears. He sings with a broken voice. And David will become a medical student years from now because he will realize that the demanding hours will save him from himself. Pablo will circle around for years before falling in with a man who is not right for him. But he will stay anyway, because that's Pablo.

We can share which of them will live quite happily: Eddie. The second Jim. Wilson and Roberto together. That will be it. They have spurious and wretched pasts, many places where time fogged over like the coastal range before San Francisco and their descents landed them in unfamiliar places. But they will remain satisfied, and none of them will ever stop in the middle of eating breakfast to think about so-and-so, why it was them and not those, those and not them. We can't learn much from them, in the end, because they will take their own reasons and swallow them as whole as snakes do eggs. Their jaws wide and open and such a looming thing disappears and is crushed and only the thin film of shell is spit out to disappear on the Valley floor.

VI

They go from club to club, and Tomás borrows money to get in and Nestor pays. At first, Tomás lingers by the doormen, as if forgetting that he has to pay, chatting, and so the ticket sellers look at Nestor and he hands them one of his hard-earned twenties.

Nestor will not take pills; he will not drink, even though Tomás tells him that the next club is only a matter of blocks, so a drink couldn't hurt. Tomás orders beer, and while he waits, he takes off his short-sleeve and stands waiting in his muscle shirt, cavalier, but here no one seems to notice. In Fresno, Nestor believes the situation between them is like something heavy in his hands. Here, we see him look around and then up at the crisscross of light and we see what kind of person Nestor really is: he names all the colors to himself. His lips move, and we can get close enough to read them: magenta, pink, red. Amber, orange, chartreuse. Sienna, yellow, green, gold. Bright white. Nestor knows colors. He keeps a sketchbook at home. He flips through the department store catalogs and writes down the names of colors. He sketches Tomás from memory. He gives them to Tomás so that Tomás knows he sketches him from memory.

He is concentrating on these lights, and if we paid attention, we would want to see just how far and deep Nestor can go with color. (We might lose ourselves in naming all the variations of blue, the way Nestor can.) So no blue—because we might not see how there are two men looking at Nestor, both of them holding drinks. They wear expensive watches and check the time, brown khakis, broadcloth shirts. We might not see them swallow hard (both of them) at what they see in Nestor. We will not get close enough to know why they are thinking what they are thinking.

VII

Tomás has a last name, but we don't think it's right to share it. He lives in Fresno, and a last name still means everything here. Down in the smaller towns, a last name can feel worse, whole streets owned by one family, the cars of all the young men crowding the front lawns.

Tomás needs to leave the Valley, and will. He has gotten himself into many situations in small towns where he has been run out of a house at gunpoint. It happened in Ivanhoe and Porterville, the back window of Nestor's borrowed car shot out once and Nestor never getting an explanation. Tomás does not know what happened to the boys he left naked and surprised in their own beds, but we know. (Of course. We know what happened to them.)

Something crowds inside Tomás that we can't recognize, even if we try. We might not understand what the old women in his family mean when they say he has tainted blood. Tainted blood is too much the metaphor for us; it can't take here. It can't work in the same way (though Nestor is the worrier, wonders what courses through his

veins). Tomás is a different, more worrisome break from our lot, holding his name back, running through with this tainted blood (a curse,
the old women say, and only some of us can sit on the lip of that
canyon and understand). Blood. Blood. Blood. Out of its element, we
can't make much sense of it, but it means much more to Tomás. It
means he cannot escape the way he is. It means he better not have
kids. It means he cannot be like the men of San Francisco (they are all
around him in this bar) who finally settle with someone after their
looks have drifted like smoke and they decide to take in an Indonesian
baby. No. This is not Tomás and is not Fresno. He is living with himself, with a land of ranchers and trucks, with hands reaching daily to
pluck the fields (so many fields, we can't know if we only buy oranges
from the corner grocer), with the birds that are housed in the small
wetlands trying to fly away from the pesticides, not dipping their
beaks into the water, as if they know that something will get in them
and cause them to lose their feathers, break apart like little downy pillows. He will leave that place. He will leave Nestor there, and we will
not know what will become of Tomás once he goes.

VIII

So Nestor and Tomás are lost in themselves in the middle of the club
lights while the men scout (as men will do in a place like this). We
will look at the two men who have been eyeing Nestor, because
Nestor is not thinking straight. He has been looking at the lights
because he saw Tomás talking to a young blond boy with too many
teeth, the boy's head tilting as if Tomás is too much to handle in
conversation and the boy is anticipating what Tomás will do to him
on his living room couch. Nestor is not looking at that (trying not
to) and so looks at the lights in anger, thinking of all the variations
of blue. We need to pay attention to these men, one of whom has
nudged the other, and they are up to no good. We look at their expensive watches and their clothes and understand how they come up
with the tiny packets of powder that they spill nervously into a bar

glass of rum and Coke. No one sees them do this, and if they did, they would think nothing of it (what's cocaine or Ecstasy or anything, anyway?) and we know that Nestor shouldn't drink that drink (Alice! Dorothy!) but the anger blooming in his chest will cause him to see one of the men and think he is a good-looking man. (We hate to admit that the men are good-looking.) We know, even through their clothes, that they are slick as seals and hard; they have fun pressing themselves against men in the bar who turn around to see what face is attached to all that muscle and aggression. We will see Nestor turn around when one taps him on the shoulder, a blond man with big hands, and Nestor will smile stupidly and take the drink. (We know what he's thinking, the self-pity that is stirred in every rum and Coke, how he'll wreck the car and Tomás in it.) We will watch him gulp it down because he doesn't know how to handle the blond man's grip on his waist and his compliments (nasty remarks, but sexy all the same), and we know we've lost him when the second man comes to join them and Nestor wilts in the face of that attention and he's a goner, the spot where he stood empty and then filled by another clubgoer. (Who cares about that one: he comes here all the time.) It's Nestor, out of the safety of the darkness of the music and the dim and shifting lights, whom we should worry about.

IX

We can call Tomás insensitive if we like. Witness: he drinks a beer and talks to the blond boy, a real New Yorker that Tomás can't understand, but it forces the two of them to step closer to each other to hear. Tomás exaggerates his own English, hobbling it with an accent here and there so that the New York boy (with a small apartment in San Francisco because he can) has to keep asking him again and again what he means. The New York boy tells him about his boyfriend in Italy, a student at an art school, and the letters that come from Rome to say sorry. Tomás listens while he drinks but doesn't ask why the New York boy is telling him any of this. Tomás knows why, of course (and so do we—a part of us knows this New York boy is naive and manipulative at the same time), that he wants Tomás in his living room and then a letter the next morning to send to Rome (the romance of thin airmail paper). We might grudgingly accept Tomás accommodating all of this, asking where the New York boy is staying, and they leave the bar and we know what will happen. Tomás has seen the two big men talking to Nestor earlier but makes nothing of it, cannot picture Nestor completing such a bargain with men like that. He leaves without much worry. But we purse our lips at Tomás and the way his head does not pivot in all directions to look for Nestor, to tell Nestor (however guiltily) that he will be back in a couple of hours, his tone implicit that they can leave the club after that to eat at a diner. He doesn't do any of that, and we know he should, because if he noticed that Nestor were nowhere to be found, his jealousy would finally surface and we would finally see, in his frantic searching of the bathroom stalls and the dance floor, that Tomás harbors a need for Nestor's sweetness, even if he never returns it.

X

Do we want to see it happening? (We know what's happening.) Do we want to enter Nestor's haze as this goes on? Or would we be better off (in the way that none of us ever wants to see the accident but wants to see the glitter of glass) seeing how Nestor will be found? Do we want to see him from afar, the dawn beginning to break over the slim alley where he will lie, and do we want to hear a sound track swelling over this sight like in the movies? (Perhaps the opening bars of "Goodbye, Yellow Brick Road," but no, Elton John is too much a sentimentalist for what happens here, and besides, Nestor and Tomás and all the rest are not children of opera and show tunes but Mexican *ranchera* in the mornings.) So we will imagine Lola Beltrán and Amalia Mendoza, the one who cries at the end of every song she sings.

How about policemen? Should we witness them as they find a very broken Nestor, his pants tossed against a Dumpster, one little black shoe lying upturned (as if he'd been hit by a car), the other still, somehow, securely on? Let's assure ourselves with the fact that both of them will approach him with their jaws dropped and that they will not call him a faggot under their breath, but they will think of their own sons at home, their own daughters.

Is it better (or worse) for us to go back a few hours and see the two men who didn't wait for Nestor to start buckling from his rum and Coke concoction? Do we want to enter that terrible space (inside those hearts and minds and bones) inside those men, who want inside Nestor? Will the parallel be too uncomfortable? And if we do get that close to that hour (it was nearly three in the morning), will we see both men, or the more brutal one, the one who wouldn't stop pressing up against Nestor even as he cried against the brick wall? What the brutal one wanted: Will we ask to hear anything more about his childhood? (He had one.) Will it serve to explain how it felt to handle this young man? (He knows his name is Nestor because Nestor said so before he drank, but when he mumbles it to himself as he pounds Nestor against the brick, he isn't saying it right.) What will we make of his enjoyment of not allowing escape, of feeling his own body control another one, his memory of kittens squirming to get rid of him and his own big hands (big hands for a kid his age) always catching little paws and tails and napes?

Will it hurt us to know that Nestor was fully aware of what was happening? (He was, broken from his daze like a gunshot, a breaking and swelling; he flashed a memory of boredom at work, the ice factory, how the ice blocks broke apart with a sudden momentum, cracks never showing in the translucence.) He felt the men and heard them and the brick wall scraping his left cheek and his own crying, his one bare foot exposed to the cold of midmorning. It is fair to say he will not remember. It would be stupid of us to think he prayed (but he did, suddenly Catholic).

Where in this picture comes the best view of what has happened? Maybe the secondary: the other man, who did the same to Nestor but in an absurdly soft and caring way. Maybe him. We won't comment on the bare bones here: he was hard, and he slipped right into Nestor after the other had done most of the work (a fish too long out of water stops flipping, not hard to hold down). But he took the time to enjoy the soft skin of Nestor's back and pulled his face away from the brick wall as if that would stop his crying. He thought he was more of the moment and he kept saying, "Relax, relax," and we will have to consider that this man actually meant what he said.

XI

In the New York boy's San Francisco apartment, Tomás has the boy naked, legs resting on his shoulders, the boy curled up to take him in. The lights are off, and we are beginning to hear snippets of dialogue. "Yeah, oh yeah, yeah," the New York boy keeps saying, but he only repeats it, so the sound of his voice makes us think we really don't need a description. The voice is sweaty and lusty and insatiable; there isn't substance to it.

It is Tomás we want to hear, isn't it? To hear him speak? To be close enough to hear his voice and how he might sound to Nestor, if it will explain anything about him. Tomás groans to his greater need, only groans and sighs. He likes the giving back of his own push inside, the resistance, then the release, and how he sees white every time that happens. But he doesn't talk during any of this; he is not one for that kind of talk.

When they are done, the New York boy says, "Do you want some water, babe?" and Tomás says yes, but he bristles at being called "babe." What we know about Tomás, though, is that he calls Nestor pet names all the time. In Spanish, he calls him *papi* and *nene* and *mono* and *chango,* and Nestor wonders what about him is monkey-like. "Monkey?" Nestor asked. (Nestor's intonation suggests that he loves the name, the question not a question, the second-guessing not second-guessing at all.) His voice is an electric spark of good intentions, clean water, flowers blooming in ridiculously bright colors. His voice is filled with love for Tomás, but we know Tomás must put up something to resist hearing it. "Monkey?" Nestor asks again (a whirl of good weather) and Tomás answers him so gently we can only be angry at him for being so kind. "Monkey, *sí*," he says, mixing Spanish and English, knowing that Nestor loves how they (and only they; can we?) do that and Tomás hugs him close, knowing that Nestor participates too much in this giving.

"Here's your water," the New York boy says, to interrupt, and the lights are still off, but if we looked as hard as Tomás does, we can see this boy's blue eyes glow in the dark, and Tomás takes a long sip. Without asking him, Tomás begins to laugh as he brings the New York boy back to the couch and they are at it again, the give-and-take, and Tomás watches the boy's eyes widen in surprise at every entry, and Tomás is mean enough to wish Nestor were there, watching this. He wants him to see how he can make this boy's blue eyes widen, how the mouth opens, and even we can't figure out what the New York boy would want to say at that exact second.

XII

We are grateful, in a strange way, that the two men have stolen Nestor's wallet. We are grateful because the policemen have ordered an ambulance to cart him away to an emergency clinic, and his injuries (kidneys: the brutal one slammed the palms of his hands on Nestor's back) require blood tests and a phone call home. They ask him where he lives, and Nestor does not want to say because his parents do not know about him, and even being in a clinic will not change that. He is awake, and we see his eyes register the possibility of his parents.

How does Tomás get there? He has been to the clinic before because once muggers stole his watch and wallet and sliced at his hands when he moved too quickly. It is the emergency clinic in the city that takes in late-night trouble. We see Tomás wander around the club at five in the morning. When he cannot find Nestor among all the bodies still threatening to rupture at so late (or early) an hour, he considers going to the usual diner. Maybe he will be there. He refused to think that Nestor would ever go home with anyone (though we can say here that Nestor has, because Nestor is much quicker about these things than Tomás, doesn't linger and continue letting anyone call him "babe"; he leaves quickly because he is shy).

But he is not at the usual diner, and on the way back to the club Tomás sees two policemen enter the doors. He asks two clubgoers outside what has happened, hoping to hear that a drug bust has gone on, but they tell him that someone had been beaten in the side alley, that an ambulance has carted him off. Tomás remembers the two men now.

He thinks of all the places to go. A police station, Nestor's parked car. He remembers the clinic and goes to a phone booth across the street from the club to call and ask if anyone has come in with a broken arm, someone short and dark, and the nurse on the other line puts him on hold. She comes back to him (we know her voice will be different, someone has told her to keep Tomás on the line), but Tomás hangs up at the first sign of hesitation.

He hails a cab to take him to the clinic, and when he arrives, we will know something more about Tomás. He is thinking ahead, in a way that will better suit him (but we know that he is convincing himself that it is for Nestor's best interest). He will sit across the street on a bus bench to see if Nestor will come out in a few hours. He wonders if Nestor will be stupid enough to give his real name so they can send him a bloated bill for whatever he got himself into. He doesn't think much of Nestor's skill at living. (But we know Nestor is already afraid, and Nestor even gives a fake name and address and says he is okay to leave.)

It isn't until nearly three in the afternoon that Nestor finally exits, and he looks determined despite his slow gait. What Tomás doesn't know is the whole story, nor that Nestor had to talk to the police, that he was swabbed and counseled, and that he eventually broke down in tears and wept harder than he ever had in his life and told them (again his voice, sad as violets), "My name is Nestor Alvarez," and gave his real address and told them, please, not to call his parents. We know that the counselors told him all about filing charges and his own willingness, but all Nestor wanted was a ride to his car so he could go home. One of the police officers gave him ten dollars so he could catch a cab because Nestor didn't want to go in a police car.

So there. All of that, as Tomás approached Nestor ready to berate him for his trouble, and Tomás doesn't know. Nestor will turn on him and begin crying, without saying just yet what happened twelve hours earlier, that late afternoon really the last time Nestor was much of anything, the beginning of the long road of remembering Tomás as the greatest of failures and of Tomás thinking that things were his fault. (Tomás can't stop the course of a story, but we want to hate him as much as Nestor does.) We will hate him as much as Nestor will for the rest of his life.

XIII

They are going home. They are on the road by five, having taken a cab back to Nestor's car, and it will be Tomás who will drive. Nestor is crying because the cuts on his cheeks will not heal in the five hours before he gets home. He is crying because he has tired of lying.

How much do we think Nestor will tell Tomás on this trip? Will he revisit the entire incident for him? Or will he break down and use it to filter himself into Tomás's life, to say (as we have done, let's not deny it) he is owed now. This horrible experience gives him claim for Tomás to take care of him. Is Nestor like that, using something like this to his advantage like George (really Jorge), who used the occasion of his mother's death to keep Tomás around? Now we know that story. (Really, Jorge.)

In fact, Nestor says very little. He says, first (that voice), "I got beat up, okay?" and then fifty miles later, after Highway 101 and crossing into that coastal range, Nestor speaks up again and says, plainly, "I got raped by two guys," and we learn much about Tomás because he does not know how to respond. He doesn't say a word for the rest of the trip and neither does Nestor. They come back into the Valley, and since we don't have anything to hear from them, we have no choice but to look at the scenery. The road twists, the diesel trucks are much slower (because they are fully loaded with tomatoes and peaches and dead chickens), and the vegetation becomes browner and drier as the elevation comes down and Tomás and Nestor descend back into the Valley. Yes, they descend, but we can't make much of that. This is simply how they got home, Tomás taking Nestor inside his house and witnessing Nestor's father having to hold back from kicking Nestor's ass for being so stupid, all that work at the ice factory gone because they wanted to go where they didn't belong. (Do we think they belong there, not here?) This might be where we will have to divide our attention, because after Tomás leaves to walk home, these two will never speak again, and we need to close the circles on them. If we stay with Nestor, we will hear the fury that boils over in this house when Nestor tells the truth (he will be kicked out that very night; it happens, even though we think we've heard it over and over). If we follow Tomás, we will see him go home and lie in his bed, and he will cry, but we can't say whether he knows why. We can't know because Tomás doesn't have a clue, either.

XIV

So what is the story? Where do we turn? What do we focus on? Who do we care about? Who do we identify with? How do we deal with Fresno? Will we come to agreement about what has really happened here? Will we see the same implications?

We want the irony or the softness, one or the other. We want the moving past of struggling with parents (because don't mothers already know, anyway?). We want to see people like Nestor and Tomás simultaneously looking at men with lust in their hearts and then not bring it into their brief mentions of life. We want them to speak Spanish on the page (because some of us like that, admit it, the dirty words you've learned) and are disappointed that they don't. We don't appreciate that this story is itching to close on an image of Nestor (still in Fresno) eating a breakfast of cereal and orange juice. Midbite, he remembers Tomás and is angry at himself because an erection greets the memory. We can tell you that this story will close with the added information that Nestor briefly dates a woman (so does Tomás, two in fact, but we will have different reactions to that). Nestor is eating breakfast. We can't know what Tomás is doing. We can't know what Nestor will do after this moment because the story wants to close.

With eating breakfast? He is eating cereal and drinking juice. He ran in the same crowd with Tyler, the Chinese American beautiful boy (who was molested by an older white man because the man found him too beautiful on his tricycle). The two men in San Francisco are in Geneva; the gentler one never did anything like that again, the other one did and never got caught. They are eating croissants in the late evening (time difference), taking bites at the same time Nestor eats his cereal (if we want it that way). How do we want it? Do we want music? Country music (because of its neutrality, in some ways, Charley Pride, just for a loop)? Not opera and (God, no) not Judy Garland. Not here. Just trumpets with a Mexican flair (yes, Mexican).

It isn't fitting. We are splitting and not agreeing because Mexican trumpets are too specific. His name is Nestor and some of us think he should levitate or endure something spiritual like that to close this story, floating right through the ceiling, sprouting wings. His name is Nestor, and don't stories with names like that need to have levitation and a good deal of magic? No, not this one. It won't. It can't. Leave him be, eating his cereal. Some of us will stay with him. Others of us won't (so go to Tomás, or Tommy, because he lets people call him that now). The rest of you can go to him on an invisible cloud. The rest of you can go see him in his new skin and bones. We will stay with Nestor and finally hear what the deal was about his dating a woman.

He will speak (if you stay or not) and you might miss his voice. He will speak about another man, too (the magnificent, if brief, Geraldo). Broken, maybe, but old bones become new bones, old skin is second skin. Flowers wilt and come back. The Valley falters, then blooms. He's eating cereal on July 1. Stay with him until the fireworks because fireworks are the greatest broken things of all (as Nestor will tell you, brilliant with color).

Clima

On a map, my mother knows home and the weather that hits it. Off the TV, she can point to California, crooked like an arm, and we can listen for rain, or Tule fog, or sun that won't stop. She doesn't know about the where of me.

New York City is just down the block. Boston is like leaning from the back porch and twisting your head to get a good look at the neighbors. A blizzard ravages Virginia or a flash flood in Maine claims six lives. She'll call, just to check I'm not one of them. There's a dusting of snow on the ground today. This worries her.

Years ago, a hurricane too wrapped up in itself to stay at the coast rushed to us. It broke apart over the Valley at two in the morning and knocked over trees and electric lines, the wooden laundry posts. It scared the cat. We all got rare sips of coffee, since the adults waited in the kitchen, the only thing working the gas stove. We had to pee in the dark, and when we got bored, we went to the windows because of the lightning—it wasn't the usual. It forked and scorched the ground, not like before, where the sky only lit up like a lot of camera bulbs. "*¡Quítense de allí!*" my mother always yelled when we neared the windows, and off we were sent to my brother's room without a view. But it was there that the house was the best—his walls had gaps in the thin planks and let in the cold, and that night, it let in the rain. Sideways, the wind egging it on. We put our hands up to the gaps on a dare, the rain needling us, making us pull back, our palms dotted red.

The sky is too gray, I tell her. I'm cold. With all the lightning, we were cold, our bedsheets draped on every mirror in every room. A reflection could blind you, my mother warned. Or set something on fire. Or blind you *and* set you on fire. And who would want that?

I worry my mother. She didn't know I put my hands to the back wall of our house to feel that rain. I tell her that today is not cold enough. That today, I want hard snow or hail falling fast enough to bounce. Ice refusing to melt, locking, jamming in.

"Ay, m'ijo," she says. *"¿Por qué dices eso?"* She grew up in Texas.

I'm opening a window, loud enough for her to hear, trying to explain that I'd sit through a typhoon, gladly let it wreck me. Because today is gray, I say. I need some kind of weather.

ABOUT THE AUTHOR

Born and raised in Dinuba, California, Manuel Muñoz attended Harvard University and Cornell University. He is the recipient of an Individual Artist Grant from the Constance Saltonstall Foundation for the Arts, and his stories have been published in *Glimmer Train Stories, Boston Review, Epoch, Colorado Review,* and many other journals. He lives in New York City.